They were on the final straight now, with just a hundred metres to go. They were the longest hundred metres Maxine had ever run. Somewhere on the straight she saw John streak past her, but she no longer cared about that. Her only thought was to force herself forward over the finish line, but she felt as if she were running through treacle. The last few steps were agony, and as she crossed the line she threw herself to the ground, gasping for air.

After a moment or two she got to her knees and pulled herself upright. 'You were right,' she said with a grimace. 'You're too fast for me.'

John didn't reply at first. He was checking the time on his watch. 'Maybe it's not working properly,' he said finally.

'What do you mean?'

'Your time. It can't be right. You did it in sixty-three seconds!'

D0414283

Don't miss the second title in the *Camp Gold* series
by Christine Ohuruogu:

CAMP GOLD: GOING FOR GOLD

CAMP GOLD

RUNNING STARS

Christine Ohuruogu
with Paul May

Tamarind Books

6284377

CAMP GOLD: RUNNING STARS 978 1 848 53093 5
A TAMARIND BOOK

First published in Great Britain by Tamarind Books,
an imprint of Random House Children's Publishers UK
A Random House Group Company

Tamarind Books edition published 2012

1 3 5 7 9 10 8 6 4 2

The Random House Group Limited supports the Forest Stewardship Council (FSC®),
the leading international forest certification organization. Our books carrying the FSC label are printed
on FSC®-certified paper. FSC is the only forest certification scheme endorsed by the leading environmental
organizations, including Greenpeace. Our paper procurement policy can be found at
www.randomhouse.co.uk/environment.

Set in Bembo

Tamarind Books are published by Random House Children's Publishers UK
61–63 Uxbridge Road, London W5 5SA

www.**randomhousechildrens**.co.uk
www.**totallyrandombooks**.co.uk
www.**tamarindbooks**.co.uk

Addresses for companies within The Random House Group Limited can be found at:
www.randomhouse.co.uk/offices.htm

THE RANDOM HOUSE GROUP Limited Reg. No. 954009

A CIP catalogue record for this book is available from the British Library.

Printed and bound in Great Britain by CPI Group (UK) Ltd, Croydon, CR0 4YY

For Mum, Dad, Obi, Charles, Victoria, Daniel,
Kingsley, Gabriel and Joshua.

CHAPTER ONE

'Hey, look!' yelled Kayle, almost bursting with excitement. 'Over there! On that banner. It says "Camp Gold"! Come on, Maxine, they're waiting for us.'

Maxine looked where her friend was pointing. Above the heads of the passengers on the crowded train station a huge banner floated. The words CAMP GOLD glittered as if they were made of actual gold, bright in the sunlight shining through the domed glass roof. As they came closer Maxine saw that there was more writing underneath: CAMP GOLD WELCOMES THE STARS OF THE FUTURE!

Despite her nervousness Maxine felt herself tingling with excitement. Her mum squeezed her hand and her three younger brothers began chanting, 'Maxine's a star, Maxine's a star,' until people around them started turning their heads to look and Maxine felt the blood rushing to her face. 'Shut up, you lot,' she hissed at her brothers. 'I'm not a star.'

'Not yet anyway,' said her mum proudly. 'But you must be special to be picked for this. Hurry up, Kayle's already there.'

They pressed forward and found about twenty girls and boys gathered underneath the banner talking excitedly. Maxine was twelve years old nearly thirteen, and she thought the others seemed to be about the same age. Standing in the midst of the throng was a tall, elegant-looking young woman with glossy, expertly cut blonde hair and the longest legs Maxine had ever seen. A gold badge on her green dress said that her name was Isabel. 'You're almost the last,' she said, a huge smile revealing perfect white teeth as she ticked off Maxine's name on her list. 'We'll be seeing a lot of each other. I'm the head gymnastics coach and I'm sure you two are in my group.'

A crowd of onlookers had gathered, all craning their necks to try and see what was going on, but now there was a sudden commotion and a small woman with very red lipstick and a red dress thrust herself forward. An enormous TV camera and several assistants were close on her heels. Before Maxine knew what was happening, the group standing beneath the banner were dazzled by brilliant lights and the lens of the camera was pointing at them.

Maxine edged backwards to stand with her

mum and her brothers as Isabel turned to speak to the Camp Gold students. 'This is a very exciting moment,' she said. 'Camp Gold is such a new and amazing place that they're going to make a whole TV show about us. Corenza would like to interview some of you, and then they'll take some shots of all of us together. Who wants to be first?'

'I know her,' said Maxine's mum suddenly. 'She's Corenza Lewis from the news. Go on, Maxine, you should let her talk to you. You'll be on TV!'

'No way!' exclaimed Maxine. 'I'm not going near those cameras, Mum.'

'Kayle's not shy,' said Joshua, who was seven years old. 'Look at her!'

Kayle had managed to push herself to the front and was smiling at the presenter, her brown eyes glittering with excitement.

'These girls and boys have come from far and

wide. They're about to climb aboard a train to go and spend three whole weeks at Camp Gold,' Corenza Lewis said to the millions of people who were watching on TV. 'Their teachers have picked them out because they have raw talent that could one day see them winning national and world records. Just one hundred and fifty kids have been given this amazing chance. Let's ask some of them how it feels. How about this young lady?' She turned to Kayle and pointed the microphone at her.

'It's just awesome,' said Kayle. 'It's the best thing that's ever happened to me.'

'And what's your sport?'

'Gymnastics,' said Kayle. 'My best friend Maxine is here too. We're just so lucky that we both got chosen!'

Maxine's mum pushed her daughter forward, and suddenly she found herself staring right into the lens of the camera. 'Amazing!' said the presenter. 'How does it feel, Maxine?'

'Um . . . er . . . great,' stammered Maxine. 'I'm really looking forward to it.'

'Terrific. Now give us a big cheer, everyone!'

The Camp Gold students all waved their arms in the air and jumped up and down, but suddenly they heard Isabel yelling over all the noise. 'Stop it, everyone! The train! It's about to leave. Grab your luggage and run!'

All around Maxine people started saying frantic goodbyes. She kissed her mum and hugged her brothers, then she was running down the platform with everyone else, trundling her suitcase behind her. 'I'm going to get you back for that,' she said to Kayle, who was running beside her. 'How could you? You knew I didn't want to.'

'We were great!' laughed Kayle. 'Just think, both of us are going to be on national TV! We're famous already, and we haven't even got to Camp Gold!'

'I don't want to be famous,' said Maxine.
'I shouldn't even be here. You know I shouldn't.
I'm sure it's all some kind of mistake.'

Kayle just laughed and threw her bag in
through the train door.

'Hey!' yelled a loud American voice. 'Watch
what you're doing with that.'

A boy appeared in the doorway. He wasn't tall
and his dark hair was cut as short as it possibly
could be. Maxine thought he looked like the
kind of boy who was used to trouble. But
suddenly his brown face was split by a wide grin.
'Just kidding,' he said. 'That little bag was
nothing. I put it up top. Here,' he said to Maxine.
'Give me yours. My name's John, by the way –
John Parravani. And in case you hadn't guessed,
I'm from the USA.'

The girls stepped onto the train and John
heaved Maxine's suitcase up onto the top shelf of
the luggage rack. Then he turned and shook

hands with both girls as they introduced themselves. 'Are people coming from all over the world, then?' asked Maxine. 'I thought—'

'Excuse? Is this right train for Camp Gold?'

They all turned at the sound of the voice. A tall, pale girl with long, curly red hair stood outside the door, looking anxiously up and down the platform. She was wearing an outsized red hooded top, flower-patterned leggings and flip-flops. Her toenails were painted green to match her eyes, and she carried a bulging red rucksack. 'I think I am late,' she said. 'Is this right train?'

'Sure,' said John. 'That's where we're going. But you'd better get aboard. I think it's about to leave.'

'Thank goodness,' cried Isabel, running towards them down the platform with her clipboard in her hand as the guard slammed the doors shut. 'You must be Alexandra Dernova, am I right? You're the very last one. Quickly, on you get.'

'Over there,' said Kayle as they entered the carriage where all the Camp Gold students were already installed. 'We can all sit together.'

Sure enough, four empty seats were waiting for them, and Maxine sank gratefully into the seat by the window. Kayle had already begun finding out everything she could about John and Alexandra. 'Where are you from, Alexandra?' she asked. 'That's the most fantastic accent.'

'I am from Russia. But you must call me Sasha. Everyone does.'

'So you and John have both come thousands of miles to go to Camp Gold?' said Kayle. 'That's incredible.'

'Well, not exactly,' said John. 'My parents live here. They were amazed when I got chosen.'

'My parents too live in this country,' said Sasha. 'This is very big chance for me. I want to win Olympic gold medal one day.'

Maxine glanced at the Russian girl and saw

that she was completely serious. 'What sport do you do?' she asked curiously, wondering if Sasha was a gymnast too.

'I am pole-vaulter. It is very dangerous sport. Very difficult. Also, I am very good at it.'

The other three began to talk excitedly to each other. Maxine saw at once that they all had one special thing in common – they all knew exactly what they wanted to do with their lives. Kayle had wanted to be a gymnast since she was three years old, and John was a runner. 'But my dad wanted me to be a football player,' he said. 'That's why he keeps buying me these T-shirts.'

John's T-shirt had the word STEELERS written across the front. 'It's spelled wrong,' said Kayle.

'Pittsburgh is where they make steel,' John said with a grin. 'That's why their football team is called the Steelers. I'm good at football, but running's the thing I love. Now I've got the chance to show my dad that I'm really good at it.'

Maxine looked out of the window as the train passed through the grimy suburbs of the city and out into the green countryside. Listening to the others talk, she thought once again that there must have been a mistake. Camp Gold was for people like Kayle. People who knew what they wanted to be. It wasn't for her. She still couldn't understand why she had been chosen. She hadn't even known that Miss Wilson, the PE teacher, had put her name forward, so the news had come completely out of the blue. She could remember it as if it were yesterday.

'We have some tremendously exciting news,' Mrs Grahame, the head teacher, had announced at the end of a very long assembly. The people around Maxine had yawned. 'Tremendously boring, she means,' Maxine's friend Lauren had whispered, and the rest of the gang had all laughed.

'I'm sure you've all heard about Camp Gold on the news,' Mrs Grahame had continued. 'I'm delighted to tell you that not just one, but two of our students have been selected for this amazing opportunity. So I'd like Kayle Devlin and Maxine Fula to come out here now.'

Maxine had remained frozen to her seat as Kayle had walked up to the front amid gasps of excitement. 'She said your name,' said an astonished Lauren. 'Go on, Maxine. It's you!'

She had walked to the front in a daze to hear Miss Wilson explaining why she had put the girls' names forward. 'I know you prefer netball and soccer,' Miss Wilson had said to Maxine afterwards, 'but you're a natural gymnast, Maxine. This is too good a chance for you to miss.'

That was easy for Miss Wilson to say, Maxine thought now as she listened to the others chattering excitedly. The trouble was, she didn't really care about gymnastics, not the way Kayle did. Kayle's eyes were shining now as she described her dream of inventing a completely new kind of twisting back-flip one day. Maxine loved sport, every kind of sport, but none of it was really serious for her, not the way it was for these others.

And there was another thing too. The rest of her friends had big plans for these holidays and she was going to miss out on everything they did. 'Kayle's your friend too,' her mum had told her, when she had grumbled about not seeing Lauren for three whole weeks. 'And anyway, I reckon it'll do you good to get away from that lot for a while. No more arguments, young lady. You're going to Camp Gold. I wish I'd had a chance like that when I was your age.'

Maxine had laughed then, because it was hard to imagine her mum ever doing any kind of sport. She smiled to herself now, and she realized that the train had slowed down and was pulling into the station.

John gave her a friendly punch on the shoulder. 'Are you always this quiet?' he asked.

She smiled and shook her head. 'I'm just a bit nervous,' she said. 'I've never done anything like this before.'

'Me neither,' said John cheerfully as they collected their luggage. They made their way out into the car park where a bus was waiting for them.

'I hope it won't take long to get there,' said Kayle. 'I'm starving!'

'Don't worry about that,' said Isabel, following them onto the bus. 'The food at Camp Gold is excellent, I promise. And we'll be there in ten minutes. If you all look out of the left-hand windows you'll have your first view of Camp Gold shortly.'

The bus drove out of the small town, then turned off the main road and made its way along a wide, tree-lined avenue. It turned a corner and suddenly, there on top of a green hill, they saw Camp Gold.

'Oh, my gosh!' exclaimed Kayle from the seat behind Maxine. 'I don't believe it!'

To their left stood a shining white mansion that had once been a luxury hotel. To the astonished students it looked like a palace. The bus drove up a long gravel drive that curved around the back of the main building, and pulled up in front of a pillared entrance. Maxine could see now that the house was just a small part of Camp Gold. Everything else was spread out below them – the brilliant red of a running track, the sparkling turquoise of a swimming pool, tennis courts and playing fields, and low modern buildings of glass and steel that Isabel told them housed gymnasiums and medical rooms and every other sports facility imaginable.

But it wasn't just the facilities that made Maxine's jaw drop in astonishment. It was everything else. Beyond the running track the land sloped away gently and she could see woods and green fields, and beyond them the deep blue of the sea.

'It's like heaven!' gasped Kayle.

'Awesome,' agreed John.

Sasha stood up. 'You know something?' she said in her strong Russian accent. 'I think we will have very good time here!'

Her green eyes glittered, and Maxine felt a sudden thrill of excitement run through her. For the moment, her doubts had vanished. Sasha was right.

This could be a whole lot of fun.

CHAPTER TWO

Maxine and her new friends gazed up in awe at the high, domed ceiling of the entrance hall. It was ribbed with gold and covered with paintings of nymphs and angels in a blue sky. Two staircases with white marble banisters curved upwards on either side of the hall, and the floor beneath their feet was tiled in intricate black and white patterns. The space around them was rapidly filling with the other students and their luggage.

'This is the old part of the house,' Isabel said. 'Leave your bags here and they'll be taken to your rooms. Follow that corridor and you'll find the restaurant.' She pointed to a passageway. 'Most of the other students have already arrived, and the principal is waiting to talk to you.'

'The principal?' said Kayle to Maxine as they walked down the corridor. 'That sounds scary.'

'Sounds like school,' said John from behind them. 'I sure hope it's not.'

An automatic door hissed open and they entered the gleaming modern restaurant. 'Well, that is not like the food we have at my school,' Sasha said, gazing hungrily at a long counter piled with an astonishing selection of good things to eat.

'Or ours,' commented Maxine, her eyes widening.

'I should think not,' said a tall black man dressed in an expensive-looking dark suit who was standing beside the food counter. Most of the tables were already full, and there was a buzz of conversation. 'The finest students deserve the finest food,' the man told them. 'Welcome to Camp Gold, everyone. My name's Michael Gladstone and I'm the principal here. Help yourselves to a bite to eat, and when you've made yourselves comfortable I'll make my little speech.' His eyes crinkled into a smile. 'Don't worry. It won't be a very long speech. I'll see you all later.'

'He's cool, isn't he?' said Kayle as they watched the principal make his way between the crowded tables to the far end of the room, pausing on the way to chat to the students. 'Cool for a teacher anyway.'

'Not as cool as this,' said John, looking at the food counter. 'And I don't think he *is* a teacher. I mean, it's not much like a school, is it? I don't know what to eat.'

'I do,' said Kayle. 'Roast chicken, and roast potatoes, and cauliflower and green beans, please,' she said to the assistant behind the counter.

Maxine chose a simple salad with strips of chicken, and she took a slice of delicious-looking apple tart to go with it. 'You'll never be able to do gymnastics if you eat like that every day,' she said, staring at the huge quantity of food that Kayle had somehow managed to get served with.

'Just watch me!' Kayle replied.

As soon as they were seated at a table, Michael Gladstone began to speak. 'I know you've all had a tiring journey,' he said. 'I just want to welcome you officially to Camp Gold. While you're here you'll have the very best of everything. The best food—' He was interrupted by a loud cheer – as Maxine was discovering, the food was truly delicious. '—the best accommodation, the best entertainment, and most important of all, the very best coaching in your chosen sport.'

There was another cheer, but the principal held up his hand for silence. 'You guys have an opportunity that most people will never have, OK? So I'll just say one thing to you all. Don't waste it.'

There was a long moment of silence as his words sank in. Maxine thought guiltily of how she had been ready to turn down the chance of coming here. But even so, she couldn't help thinking that there must be other people who deserved it more than she did.

'OK,' said Michael Gladstone after a pause. 'That's the serious stuff over. I know you're all going to work hard. When you leave here you're free to go to your rooms and explore Camp Gold for yourselves. Then, at seven o'clock, we have a special visitor. I'm sure you've all heard of Danny Crowe . . .' There was a burst of excited conversation. Danny was the country's most

famous athlete. He had won four Olympic gold medals. 'Danny's going to set the scene for your three weeks here,' Michael Gladstone continued. 'Make sure you're on time. That's all, folks.'

When they returned to the entrance hall their luggage had vanished. They found plastic smart cards laid out on a table with their names and room numbers printed on them. 'Girls' rooms are up the stairs and to the left,' said a smiling woman, who was seated behind the table. 'Boys' rooms are on the ground floor in the new wing, down that corridor there.'

The girls arranged to meet John in half an hour, and headed up the grand curving staircase. They came to Maxine's room first. She slid her card into the lock and pushed the door open and the three girls stepped inside. Maxine was speechless. She crossed the thick carpet to the open window and looked out over the sports fields to the sea. She turned and her eyes took in the comfortable bed, the framed action photographs of sports stars on the walls, and another door. She opened it and found a bathroom, complete with a fluffy white bathrobe and a pile of white towels. 'Hold on!' she exclaimed. 'There's only one bed, does that mean . . . ?'

'Yup, it's all yours,' said Isabel, coming into the room. 'Didn't you hear what Michael said? Here at Camp Gold you have the best of everything.'

The other two girls ran off down the corridor to find their own rooms. 'Enjoy it!' Isabel told Maxine with a smile, closing the door.

Maxine was alone at last. She kicked off her shoes and lay down on the bed. The sound of birdsong drifted in through the window, along with a murmur of wind in the trees. Maxine thought of the cluttered bedroom at home that she shared with her older sister, Lola. She thought of the tiny bathroom that seven people had to share. And now she had one all to herself! She could take a bath whenever she liked. Maybe she should take a shower now. It was a good thought, but first she would close her eyes for a moment . . .

She was woken with a start by a loud knocking on her door. 'Hey, Maxine, come on! We're going out to explore, remember?'

Maxine glanced at her watch. She'd been asleep for only ten minutes, but she felt refreshed. 'OK,' she called. 'I'm coming.'

She ran into the bathroom and splashed cold water on her face, then pulled on her trainers and opened the door. Sasha and Kayle were standing there, huge smiles on their faces. 'Our rooms are just like yours,' Kayle said, peering into her friend's room. 'Come on, we'll be late.'

They ran down the curving staircase and out onto the wide gravelled area outside the main door. The bus had gone, and Maxine saw that the place where it had been parked was really a kind of terrace, bordered by a stone balustrade from which they could look down over all Camp Gold's facilities. John was waiting for them, sitting on the stone ledge. 'This is like the kind of hotel you see on TV,' he said, jumping down. 'Have you guys ever been anywhere like this before?'

They all shook their heads. 'I never even knew there *were* places like this,' Maxine said.

They walked off together down a broad path that led to the running track. They passed other students as they went, most of them with slightly dazed expressions on their faces. They examined the track, and the outdoor swimming pool, and they peered in through the windows of the gym and the treatment rooms. 'Did you ever see so many machines?' Kayle said as they walked away from the gym. 'I can't imagine what you do on most of them.'

'There's another pool,' exclaimed Maxine. 'An indoor one. It's massive!'

'And look,' said Sasha. 'They have a sauna and a Turkish bath. Unbelievable!'

'They have basketball too,' exclaimed John, turning a corner into a secluded courtyard. A basketball hoop was fixed to a high, windowless brick wall that Maxine decided must be the back of the gym block, and a half-court was marked out on the tarmac. 'All we need now is a ball,' John said. 'Maybe they keep one around here some place.'

On two sides the courtyard was bounded by a wire fence, but on the third there was a low white building with several doors to it. John tugged at the first door, but it was locked.

'Do you think you should?' asked Kayle anxiously.

'Sure,' said John, trying the second door. 'Why not? They told us we could go where we liked. If there's a basketball hoop they must mean for us to play ball, right?' He tugged at the next door and gave a grunt of satisfaction as it opened. 'See?' he said, leaning in through the door and emerging with an orange basketball in his hands. 'I knew it!'

He tossed the ball underhanded towards Maxine. It left his hand fast and flew way too high. 'Hey, sorry . . .' he began, but Maxine reacted instinctively, leaping high and grabbing the ball out of the air with one hand. 'Let's have a game, then,' she said, laughing at the startled expression on John's face. 'Me and Kayle against you two, OK? It'll be an international! Britain against the rest of the world.'

She threw the ball to Kayle, who bounced it a couple of times then glanced up at the hoop and threw an arcing shot that dropped through without even touching the rim.

'I bet you can't do that again,' said John as Maxine retrieved the ball.

'You don't think so?' said Kayle. 'Just watch me!'

Maxine laughed. She and Kayle played together most nights on the small court by the flats. They were better than most of the local boys and Kayle was deadly with a standing shot. 'OK,' said Maxine. 'Let's play.'

She moved to pass to Kayle, but suddenly Sasha was in front of her. The Russian girl was fast and fluid in her movements, and her reach was long. She intercepted Maxine's attempted pass and flung the ball hard at John, who took it easily and moved towards the basket with a fast, controlled dribble. He was about to shoot when they were interrupted by a shout from far side of the court.

'Hey! Who said you could play on here?'

There were three of them – two girls and a

boy. It had been the boy who had shouted. He was tall, with dark hair parted on one side that flopped over one eye. One of the girls was black and nearly as tall as the boy, with her hair braided in corn-rows. The other girl was small and blonde. They all wore tracksuits and trainers, and a quick glance told Maxine that their gear was expensive. Very expensive.

John stepped forward, still bouncing the ball. 'I guess it was Michael Gladstone who said we could play here. Leastways, he told us we could go where we liked. Is that OK with you guys?'

'We just don't want you to get in any trouble on your first day,' said the black girl. Her accent, like her clothes, was expensive. 'We come here every week, you see.'

'Our school is allowed to use the facilities, actually,' said the smaller girl. 'And our parents pay quite a lot of money for us to come here.'

'What? Not like us, you mean?' asked Kayle angrily. 'We've got as much right to be here as you have, and I wouldn't want to go to your swanky school anyway. You're probably not even meant to be here, not now Camp Gold has taken over.'

'Well, that's where you're wrong,' said the boy. 'We're the nearest school to Camp Gold and we got three special invitations. We were the three lucky ones. And we're telling you, you can't play on here, and you definitely can't use that basketball. Where did you get it anyway?'

'You know what?' said John. 'If it's such a big deal, why don't you go find one of the coaches? We're cool with that, right, guys?'

'Sure,' said Maxine.

'Good idea,' said Kayle, looking the boy directly in the eye.

'Forget it, Oliver,' said the black girl. 'Let them get in trouble if they want to. Why should we care?'

'Yes, right,' said Oliver, backing off. 'You can't say we haven't warned you.'

John laughed as they started to walk away. 'Why don't you stay?' he called after them. 'Have a game? No hard feelings, right?'

Just for a second the black girl turned and caught Maxine's eye, then the smaller girl tugged at her arm and muttered something to her and the three of them disappeared round the corner of the building.

'Good,' said John. 'I didn't want to play with them anyway. Game on!' He dribbled swiftly towards the basket, leaped high and planted the ball through the hoop.

'That's not fair,' yelled Kayle. 'We weren't ready.'

The game continued, fast and furious, and Maxine was soon completely absorbed. They played on, point after point, as the sun dipped behind the roof of the gym block and left the basketball court in shadow. They played on as the orange light of a sunset flooded across the woods and fields beyond Camp Gold.

They played on until John suddenly froze with the ball in his hands. 'Oh, no!' he breathed.

The others turned, and saw the principal walking towards them, with the unmistakable figure of Danny Crowe by his side.

CHAPTER THREE

Maxine couldn't move. She exchanged horrified glances with the others. She didn't need to look at her watch to know that they had missed Danny Crowe's talk completely.

The two men were still walking towards them, deep in conversation, but now, as they came out of the last of the sunlight and into the shadow, they saw the four students standing there and they stopped dead. There was a long moment's

silence. Michael Gladstone looked at them
sternly.

'I assume that you lot have been out here the
whole time?' he said. 'You missed the
introductory talk?'

'I'm sorry, Mr Gladstone,' John said. 'It was my
fault. We were exploring and we found the ball
and I guess we got carried away. We forgot the
time.'

'We don't do anything here at Camp Gold
without a good reason,' Michael Gladstone said.
'Danny has given up his time to come here and
talk to you and you should show respect by
turning up to listen to him. I hope you aren't
planning to miss training whenever you feel like it.'

'No way,' said Maxine. 'We're sorry, truly.'

'OK, then,' said the principal, looking at them
carefully. 'Make sure it doesn't happen again.'

There was a pause, and then Danny's face
cracked into a grin. 'Hey, man,' he said to

Michael. 'At least they were doing sport. That is what we brought them all here to do after all.'

'I guess that's true,' said Michael Gladstone, a small smile slowly creeping onto his face. 'I'd rather be shooting some hoops myself than sitting inside listening to you talking.'

'What do you mean?' retorted Danny. 'It was a brilliant speech. I was incredible.'

'You were good,' agreed Michael. 'But now I'm going to whip you at basketball. Except our ball has been stolen.' He looked at the group with a twinkle in his eyes.

'I'm sorry, Mr Gladstone,' said John sheepishly. 'We . . . we thought it would be OK.'

The principal smiled. 'It's OK, I'm only teasing. Why don't you guys stay and play a game with us?'

'Are you any good?' asked Danny. 'Think you could beat us?'

A glint appeared in John's eye. 'You mean four

of us against you two? It wouldn't be fair. One of us can play on your side.'

'No way,' said Michael, smiling broadly. 'We'll take you on alone, right, Danny? Throw me that ball, young man. What's your name?'

By the time the light faded and it was too dark to play, the scores were even at fifteen points each, and Maxine found to her amazement that she was calling the principal of Camp Gold by his first name, and she was talking to Danny Crowe as if he were an old friend.

'So what do we have here?' Danny asked as he pulled a hoodie over his T-shirt. 'Runners, throwers, what are you all?'

'I am pole-vaulter,' Sasha declared proudly before the others could speak.

'And I'm a sprinter,' said John. 'Four hundred metres is my best distance.'

Danny nodded and turned to the Kayle and Maxine. 'How about you two?'

'I'm a gymnast,' said Kayle. Maxine couldn't speak, so Kayle answered for her. 'We both are.'

'Well, you've all come to the right place,' Danny said. 'Michael here was my coach when I was your age, and look where he got me. And he was a good four-hundred-metre runner himself, you know, when he was younger. He's a little out of shape now, though, or we'd have beaten you guys easily.'

'Me, out of shape?!' retorted Michael indignantly. 'I could take you over four hundred right now!'

Danny laughed. 'Seriously,' he said to the four friends. 'All the coaches here are top people. You'll never have a better chance to make your mark, OK? You impress people here and you could all be going right to the top. That's if you want it bad enough.'

'The other thing you would have heard from Danny if you'd been there,' Michael said, 'is that we've arranged a competition for you at the end of the three weeks. You'll be competing against some top junior internationals and we'll all be able to see how much progress you've made.'

'You'll be on TV too,' Danny said. 'It's a great way to let people see what you can do, and good practice at giving your best performance under pressure. Just remember that Camp Gold athletes are special. You must be, or you wouldn't be here.'

'But the next time you have an important meeting to attend,' Michael said, looking serious again, 'you make sure you're there on time, right? Missing Danny's performance is no big deal. But be late for your coaching, or for any of the other good stuff we have laid on for you, and we might get to thinking you're disrespecting Camp Gold. You understand?'

'We will be very good students,' said Sasha, rolling her r. 'We promise.'

They all hastened to agree. 'And now you'd

better get to bed,' Michael said. 'It's getting late if you don't watch out you'll be breaking the curfew.'

When Maxine's alarm woke her the following morning, she switched it off and lay in her wonderfully comfortable bed for a few moments listening to the sound of birds outside her window. Her phone buzzed on the table and she picked it up to see a text from her mum on the screen: **Good luck, Maxine. We're all thinking of you. Knock them dead! x**

She smiled. She'd called home the night before and told her parents just a little of what had happened since she'd left them at the train station. Already it seemed like years ago. She got out of bed, showered and dressed and went down to breakfast. She felt nervous. She couldn't help it. And even though the food was as delicious as ever, she could only pick at some cereal. Kayle didn't seem worried at all, and was happily tucking into bacon and tomatoes, but Maxine was very surprised to see that John was looking anxious.

'I guess I'll be OK,' he said. 'But I was thinking about what Danny said to us. This is going to be fun, but it doesn't sound like it'll be easy.'

'It would not be good if it was easy,' said Sasha seriously. Then she smiled mischievously. 'But we can have fun after, I think.'

They all laughed and Maxine felt a little better. When breakfast was over she and the others sat outside in the sunshine for half an hour and chatted until it was time for classes to begin. Then she and Kayle made their way to the gymnastics hall, where they found a group of about twenty students gathered.

Isabel was there, and they were all watching a gymnast going through a routine on the rings on the far side of the gym. The muscles on his arms stood out as he held himself in a perfect handstand before working through several other moves and dismounting with a perfect triple somersault. The students applauded as he walked over to join them, hardly out of breath. 'This is Boris, everyone,' Isabel told them. 'He's an excellent coach, but he is a bit of a show-off.'

Boris laughed. He was pale-faced and dark-haired with black stubble on his cheeks and chin. 'Let's do a gentle warm-up,' he said. 'Everyone spread out on the floor and we'll start with some stretches. Then in a little while we have a nice surprise for you.' He clapped his hands. 'Let's get to work.'

As she made her way onto the floor, Maxine bumped into the tall black girl in front of her. 'Sorry,' she began. Then she stopped. 'Oh,' she said. 'It's you.'

It was the girl from the night before on the

basketball court. She gave Maxine a hard stare, then turned away. And as they began the exercises Maxine soon had to concentrate so hard that she forgot all about the incident. Half an hour later she and Kayle were lying side by side on the floor, letting their muscles relax. 'If that's his idea of a gentle warm–up,' Kayle said, 'I hate to think what's coming next.'

'Wait,' said Maxine. 'I think we're about to find out.'

A grey-haired woman had appeared in the doorway, wearing a black dress and a long pink scarf. She was limping slightly, and carried a wooden walking stick. 'Over here, everyone,' called Isabel. 'I'd like you to meet Madame Farage. She's from the National Ballet Academy and she's going to give you a ballet class every day.'

Maxine groaned before she could stop herself, and Isabel heard her. 'I know,' she said. 'Ballet is hard, but those dance elements in your floor routines are important. We'll be having jazz dancers and street dancers in to help us too, but we'll also be having a ballet class every day. So let's get started.'

Maxine had tried ballet classes when she was younger. It was OK, but it wasn't really her thing. She gritted her teeth and did her best, but she knew she was no good at it. Madame Farage was full of praise for Kayle, though, and for the girl from the basketball court, whose name turned out to be Tamsin. 'This is formidable,' she said to both of them. 'Maybe you should give up this gymnastics nonsense and come to train with me!'

'Don't you dare,' said Isabel, laughing. 'OK now, everyone. Take a five-minute break and then we're going to do some vaulting.'

'At last,' Maxine said to Kayle. 'Something I can actually do.'

'Really?' said Tamsin. 'I'm looking forward to seeing that.'

'What do you mean?' asked Maxine, hearing the sarcasm in her voice.

'Forget it,' said Kayle. 'She's not worth bothering about. I bet her parents paid for her to have hundreds of ballet lessons. Let's get over there. I heard one of the others say that the vault is Isabel's best event. I want to see what she's going to teach us.'

They made their way over to the vaulting runway. 'Let's start with a straightforward hand-spring,' Isabel said. 'Are you all happy with that?'

'Sure,' said Tamsin, stepping forward. She launched herself down the runway and executed a handspring with a piked dismount that looked absolutely perfect to Maxine. She saw Isabel nodding approval. She could see from the faces of the others around her that they were all keen to show what they could do, and now she suddenly felt nervous again. When her turn came she produced a vault that was nothing like her best. She was annoyed with herself, and for the rest of the morning she worked extra hard, but the harder she worked, the worse she seemed to do.

'Relax!' Isabel said, taking her to one side when they broke for lunch. 'That's all it is, you know. You're trying too hard.'

'What did she say?' asked Kayle as the girls walked through to the restaurant.

'She told me to relax. I wish it was that easy.'

Kayle was sympathetic. 'I think we're going to do some tumbling this afternoon,' she said. 'That's your best thing.'

'I thought vaulting was my best thing,' said Maxine gloomily. 'Look, there are Sasha and John.'

They joined their friends at the table. Maxine didn't need to ask if they'd had a good time. They were both glowing. As they all moved to the food counter, Michael came by.

'Hi, guys,' he said. 'Not too worn out after that licking we gave you last night?'

'I thought it was the other way round,' said John, raising his eyebrows.

Michael laughed. 'We'll have to do it again sometime. Right now, I've got to rush. See you later.' Then he was off again, weaving through the crowded restaurant. He sat down beside Isabel at a table by the window.

'I can't believe the people who work here are all so friendly,' John said, helping himself to a large bowl of pasta.

'It is true,' said Sasha. 'They are not like teachers at all.'

'Not any teachers I've ever had anyway,' Maxine agreed. 'Miss Wilson's nice — for a teacher, but you couldn't talk to her like you can talk to Michael.'

'Isabel's talking to him all right,' Kayle said. 'I wonder what they're being so serious about? He came into the gym to see her twice this morning, and I was sure she blushed the second time.'

'You don't think . . . ?'

Maxine glanced over to the window, where Michael was leaning forward in his seat, listening as Isabel spoke.

'Who knows?' said Kayle. 'It's possible. We'll have to keep an eye on them, won't we?'

They all laughed. When they had finished eating they went outside and sat together in the shade of a giant cedar tree. Kayle asked John how come he was in this country and not back in the USA. John started to tell them about his father's job, and Maxine lay down and let the conversation wash over her. Whatever happened, she thought, she had made some great new friends. Maybe this afternoon would be better.

But she was wrong about that. It started straight away as Isabel showed them a balance that looked easy, but was very hard to hold.

Maxine felt herself wobbling. 'She's a jelly baby,' said a voice behind her in a whisper that was meant to be heard. 'She shouldn't even be here.'

Maxine made another attempt at holding the balance. It was no good. After a couple of seconds she had to give up. 'See?' whispered Tamsin nastily. 'She can't hack it.'

She's right, Maxine thought miserably. What am I going to do? I just look stupid.

'Don't worry about it, Maxine,' Isabel said quietly, coming to her side. 'It happens to all of us, believe me. You're probably just tired from all that excitement yesterday.'

'But I'm not. I just don't think I can do it.' Maxine felt the tears coming, and there was nothing she could do to stop them. She wiped them angrily away. 'I shouldn't be here. I'm no good at this. I'm sorry.'

She ran from the room, her eyes blinded by tears.

CHAPTER FOUR

Maxine ran down the corridor and out into the sunshine. She leaned against a wall, then sank to the ground and sat with her head in her hands. A few moments later Isabel joined her and sat down beside her. She put a hand on her shoulder. 'It's not as bad as you think it is,' she said.

'Yes, it is,' sniffed Maxine. 'I'm not good enough to be here. I know it, and they all know it too.'

'You wouldn't be here if you weren't good enough,' Isabel said. 'Anyone can see that you have talent. Michael says you're a terrific basketball player.'

Maxine looked up. So they'd been talking about her. Maybe that was what they'd been talking about at lunch time. It wasn't a pleasant thought. 'I'm good at gymnastics too,' she said. 'Or I was until today. But I don't care about it like Kayle does. I'd rather play basketball or soccer.'

'Well, you can still do all of them, can't you? But gymnastics is what you came here for. You really should try and make the most of it. Don't come back inside now. Take a walk. Enjoy this lovely sunny day and have a think. I bet you'll feel different in the morning.'

Isabel went back inside. Maxine stood up. She didn't know what had come over her back in the gym, but she couldn't have, stayed there a moment longer with all of them looking at her like that. She could just imagine them all talking about her now. *That crazy girl*, they'd be saying. She could hear Tamsin's voice in her head as she walked down the grassy path towards the running track: *She shouldn't even be here.*

Saska stopped. A bunch of runners jogged past ahead of her and she saw John at the back of the group. As she watched, he sprinted to the front of the line and then settled again to his original, steady pace. Moments later the runner who was now at the back moved forward to the front with a quick burst of speed. John looked up and saw her, gave her a quick wave, then focused again on the track ahead of him.

Away to her left Maxine saw a sudden flash of movement and she turned to see a pole-vaulter climb impossibly high into the air and twist over the bar before falling to land on her back on a massive foam landing pad. The vaulter jumped to her feet, punching the air. Maxine looked for Sasha, and saw her standing with a group at the end of the runway. Then the group broke up and Sasha picked up a pole, flexed it and moved to the start of the track.

Maxine moved closer, fascinated. Sasha seemed to be talking to herself as she prepared to vault, rocking backwards and forwards, her eyes fixed on the end of the runway where Maxine saw a box in the ground, midway between the poles that held the bar high above, surrounded by more heavy padding.

Sasha rocked backwards one last time, and then she ran. Maxine could see that, just like the vault in the gym, you had to generate speed on the run-up. Sasha planted her pole with a crunch into the box and she started to climb. But even Maxine's unpractised eye could see that it was all going wrong. Halfway up, while the pole was still flexing and Sasha was lying backwards she let go of the pole and flew under the bar, landing awkwardly on the landing pad as the bar and her pole both crashed down on top of her.

'That looked painful,' Maxine said, going over to join her as she picked up her pole.

'Not so bad,' Sasha said with a rueful smile. 'My run-up was wrong, that's all. I will get it right next time, I think.'

Saska made her way back to where the coach was standing and exchanged a few words with her before moving a marker at the side of the runway. Maxine settled down to watch. The pole-vaulters seemed to be completely fearless. They had to be sprinters and gymnasts at the same time, and this looked a lot more dangerous than anything Maxine had ever seen inside a gym. Finally, it was Sasha's turn again. She ran up with the same determined look on her face. It all looked good to Maxine, and this time Sasha was much closer, but still the bar came crashing down.

Sasha made three more attempts before she finally rose like a bird and sailed over the bar with what looked like half a metre to spare. Maxine stood up and applauded. Sasha flashed a grin at her, then turned and made her way back to the end of the runway and prepared to go again.

Maxine made her way thoughtfully back to her room. If Sasha could do that after a series of failures, then maybe she could make it in the gym too.

The next day started well. Isabel was great. She didn't make a fuss about Maxine's return, just gave her a friendly nod of the head. And although Maxine could see the others looking at her curiously, she worked hard all morning. She gritted her teeth and tried to point her toes and turn out her feet in the ballet class, and she made a much better job of all the drills they went through. She even managed to ignore all Tamsin's barbed comments and concentrate instead on the friendly words of the other girls.

It was after the lunch break that things went wrong. She came back into the gym with Kayle, and instantly heard Tamsin's voice. 'I can't imagine why she ever got selected,' she was saying to a small group gathered just inside the door. 'She's obviously not good enough. There are half a dozen girls at my school who deserve it more than she does.'

'Maxine, no!' Kayle tried to grab her friend's arm, but Maxine shook it off angrily.

'I'm sick of this,' she said, pulling another girl out of the way and facing up to Tamsin. 'If you've got something to say, why don't you say it to my face? You've been whispering behind my back all morning, and I've had enough!'

'All right, I will. You—'

'That'll do!' Isabel came through the door and placed herself between the two girls. 'I don't know what it is with you two, but it stops right now, OK?'

'It wasn't Maxine's fault,' Kayle began, but Isabel held up a hand.

'Whatever it was,' she said, 'you can sort it outside. I won't have you bringing personal things in here. We're here to work, and that's what we're going to do.'

'I'm aching all over,' said Kayle an hour later as they walked back to their rooms after the session was over. 'I think she made us work harder because she was cross.'

'Don't worry,' said Maxine grimly. 'I won't do that again.'

'Good,' said Kayle. 'I'm going to soak in a hot bath. How about going for a swim later?'

'Maybe. I don't know. I'll see how I feel.'

'Hey, cheer up. You did good today.'

'It doesn't feel like it,' Maxine replied. 'I'll see you later, OK?'

Alone in her room, Maxine picked up her phone and stared at it for a moment before calling home. Her little brother Joshua answered, and instantly her eyes filled with tears. 'Hey, Joshua,' she said. 'Is Mum there?'

'We watched you on TV,' Joshua told her. 'You were OK, but Kayle was better.'

She smiled through her tears. Joshua always told it the way he saw it. 'Oh, right,' she said. 'Thanks a million, Joshua!'

'That's OK. I'll get Mum.'

He put the phone down, and Maxine could hear the familiar sounds of her home: boys arguing somewhere; the TV on, and in the background the sound of her sister's new favourite band. Then her mum was there.

'Hey, Maxine. How's it going?'

There was a long silence. Then Maxine said: 'Mum, I want to come home.'

'Hey, love, don't cry. Tell me what's the matter.'

Once Maxine had started, she couldn't stop. She poured out all her doubts about not being good enough. She told her mum how she'd made a fool of herself in the gym sessions. 'I don't belong here, Mum,' she said. 'Can't you just come and bring me home? Please?'

'Hey, listen,' her mum said when she finally stopped. 'I'm sure it can't be as bad as all that. Last time you called it was the most amazing place you'd ever been. It can't have changed that much, can it? You've had a bad day, honey, but we all have them sometimes.'

'You don't understand, Mum—'

'Besides, how am I going to come and get you? Your father's away working, and what would I do with your brothers? You're miles away, Maxine. I can't just drop everything and come and get you.

I'll tell you what, you give it until the weekend. If things aren't better by then, well, I suppose you'll have to come home.'

Maxine put the phone down. She didn't think she could face another hour, let alone the rest of the week. Then she had an idea. She had money. Maybe she could get the train? It wasn't far to walk into town. She could leave a note so they wouldn't worry, and she could ring home once she was safely on the train, then there would be nothing anyone could do about it.

She felt better at once. She tore a sheet of paper from her notebook and was about to start writing when she heard voices outside the door and there was a loud knocking.

John, Sasha and Kayle all bundled into her room. 'Get your swimming things,' Sasha said, her big eyes shining. 'We are going to swim in the sea before the movie this evening.'

'I still think we should just go to the pool,'

said Kayle, looking worried. 'You know they said we weren't to go off the site.'

'It's an adventure,' said John. 'We've all been working hard. We're allowed to have a good time too. They'll never even know we were gone. Come on, Maxine, what do you say?'

Maxine looked at John and Sasha's expectant faces. Even if they got caught, she thought, what harm could it do? She was going to leave anyway.

'Sure, why not?' she said, grabbing a towel and her costume.

'Yes!' John gave her a high five. 'See, Kayle? If Maxine's not worried, what's the problem?'

'Come on, Kayle,' Maxine said. 'You know you want to!'

Kayle grinned suddenly. 'All right, then. What are we waiting for? Who knows the way?'

They walked through the grounds, past the running track and through an ornamental garden. At the end of a long grassy walk there was a high brick wall with a small green gate in it.

'That's it!' said John. 'When I was on a break this afternoon I saw two of the coaches leave that way.'

He took hold of the catch and pulled the door open. Beyond the door they could see a path following the edge of a small wood. The sea looked much closer from here. They were about to go through when they heard voices behind a nearby hedge.

'Wait,' whispered Kayle. 'I think it's Michael and Isabel. I want to hear what they're saying.' She put a finger to her lips and moved closer to the hedge. The others followed her silently.

'It was such a stupid thing to do,' Isabel was saying. 'I can't believe I did it!'

'Don't worry, really. I bet it's not as bad as you think.'

'You know it is. Everyone's going to find out. I'm sure they are . . .'

'Hey, don't worry, OK? I'll have a word. I'll fix it. Now, I have to get back. Are you coming?'

'Quick,' hissed Maxine. 'Through the wall.' She could hardly contain her excitement. 'What's she done?' she said to the others, her eyes wide as they shut the door safely behind them. 'It sounds like she's done something terrible.'

'Yeah, but Michael's going to help her,' said Kayle. 'So now they're both in it together. Oh my God, it's awful!'

'Is probably terrible crime,' said Sasha, rolling her eyes. Her accent always became stronger when she was excited.

John laughed. 'You all have crazy imaginations,' he said. 'She's made some kind of mistake and Michael's her boss so he's going to sort it out. I bet it's no big deal. And it's none of our business either. Come on, let's go swim.'

CHAPTER FIVE

Waves broke lazily along the golden sand. The summer had been long and hot, and the water was clear and almost warm. They stayed in for a long time, diving through the breakers and splashing about in the shallows. 'What time does the movie begin?' Kayle asked idly as the girls changed behind some rocks.

'Seven o'clock,' replied Sasha, towelling her long hair dry.

Kayle picked up her watch, looked at it and gasped. 'We're going to be so late,' she said. 'It's a quarter to now. We'll never make it.'

Maxine was feeling better than she'd felt all day. If only Camp Gold was all swimming in the sea and fooling around with her friends. But it wasn't. And however little she cared about being late back, she knew the others did. 'It'll be OK,' she said, rolling her damp costume in her towel. 'We can take a short cut. The field with the cows, remember?'

Although Camp Gold was not far from the sea, the path had followed a circuitous route to the beach and there was definitely a quicker way back. They made their way through the sand dunes and along a narrow path for a short distance before arriving at a gate. Cows were grazing placidly on the other side of the fence.

'You see?' said Maxine. 'You can actually see

the wall up there. It's really near. We just have to climb over two gates.'

'Cool,' said John. 'Why not? There's no point being late if we don't have to be.'

'Let's do it then,' said Maxine, and she vaulted neatly over the gate.

Kayle laughed as she followed her. 'That's the best vault you've done all day,' she said.

They walked carefully across the field. It was huge, and there were large green cowpats everywhere. 'Ugh!' said Kayle. 'I seriously do not want to step in one of them. My trainers would be totally ruined.'

The cows ignored them completely, hardly even looking up from the serious business of munching grass. They were halfway across the field when Sasha stopped and said, 'Look over there. That is very enormous cow, I think.'

They all turned to look. 'That's not a cow,' said John, his voice suddenly urgent. 'That's a bull, and it's coming this way. We should make ourselves scarce.'

The bull was lumbering slowly up from the bottom of the field towards them. Its massive shoulders swayed from side to side, but it was the enormous pointed horns that drew all their eyes. They turned and ran up the slope towards the gate. Kayle gave a cry of annoyance as her trainer landed right in the middle of a cowpat, but she hardly broke her stride. John reached the gate first and held out a hand to help the girls over.

'Wait,' said Maxine. 'Where's Sasha?'

'There!' said John. 'Oh no! She's fallen!'

Away down the field Sasha was struggling to her feet. Maxine didn't hesitate. She flew back down the field and helped her up. The bull was much closer now, and suddenly it began to move faster. 'Quick!' exclaimed Maxine. 'It's coming after us.'

The two girls took to their heels. They raced

full-tilt for the gate, and one after another they vaulted over it. The bull shuddered to a halt and stood staring at them with brown eyes. It pawed the ground a couple of times with its hoof, then turned and ambled slowly away.

'That was just too close!' said Maxine, breathing hard.

'Thank you,' gasped Sasha. 'When I fell over I thought I was finished.'

'You could have been in trouble there,' said a deep voice behind them. Michael Gladstone was walking towards them down the path from Camp Gold. 'I was watching you from the gate. It's really silly to try walking across any field with livestock in it if you don't know what you're doing. I suppose you've been swimming?'

They all nodded. 'We didn't know there was a bull,' Maxine said. 'I thought they were supposed to have signs.'

'No. They have gates and fences instead. They

expect people to be sensible and follow the path.'

'Sorry, Michael,' they all said together. It was clear that they were all embarrassed. Sasha had turned a bright shade of pink.

He shook his head. 'Listen, you guys can't just go wandering off wherever you like, you know. We don't keep that gate locked during the day because we want to be able to trust you, OK? If it's a holiday on the beach you want, then you should get your parents to take you. You came here to turn yourselves into top-class athletes, right?' They all nodded. 'Well, I'd like you to show us what you can do on the track and in the gym and over that pole-vault bar,' he said. 'And no more racing with bulls.' He looked sharply at Maxine. 'I thought you told me you were a gymnast,' he said.

'I did. I mean, I am.'

'Hmmm. I just watched you run up that field, and back down again and then back up to the gate. You were hardly out of breath.'

Maxine didn't know what to say.

'And then there was that basketball game. The rest of them were all looking tired, but you were as fresh as a daisy!'

The others started to protest. 'I could have kept going,' John said.

'Well, I don't think I could,' Michael replied. 'And despite what Danny said, I reckon I'm as fit as any of you. Except Maxine, maybe. You should think about that, Maxine. And now you guys had better get going. The movie starts in three minutes. You might just make it if you run!'

Michael walked off down the path towards the beach with a bouncy stride. The words of a song floated back to them.

'He's singing!' John said. 'I thought we were going to be in big trouble there. Lucky for us he's in such a good mood.'

'There was something on his cheek,' Sasha said

thoughtfully as they walked towards the green door in the wall. 'Did you see? A red mark.'

'Ooooh!' exclaimed Kayle. 'I know what happened. It must have been lipstick! He was helping out Isabel, right? And she was really grateful so she must have given him a kiss! I bet that's what happened. And now they'll fall in love. It's just so-o perfect.'

'You know what?' said John with a grin. 'He most probably cut himself shaving. Or he's got some kind of a rash.'

'No way!' said Maxine.

'You are so boring,' Kayle said to John.

'Yeah? Well, there's something else. Isabel doesn't wear lipstick. Hadn't you noticed?'

Kayle threw her wet towel at John's head, but he dodged neatly and ran off towards the main doors of the hotel block. When he reached them he stopped and waited for the others to catch him up.

'I've been thinking,' he said. 'I don't really feel like sitting inside and watching a movie. I'm going to go down to the track and do some work. Any of you want to come too?'

'You're kidding,' said Kayle. 'It's the new Jake Carson movie. I mean, it's not even in the cinemas yet.'

'I love Jake Carson,' Sasha said wistfully. 'I do not wish to miss this movie.'

'How about you, Maxine?' asked John. 'Maybe Michael was trying to say he thought you might be a runner. It could be true.'

Maxine was startled. Had that really been what Michael had been saying?

'Don't listen to him,' said Kayle, laughing. 'I'll see you in the movie room.'

She and Sasha headed off to their rooms. Maxine was still standing on the steps. 'Come down to the track if you want,' John said. 'I'll be there for a while.'

Maxine went up to her room, thinking hard about what John had said. She hung up her wet towel and swimming costume and sat down on her bed. It was worth a try, wasn't it? She knew she could run fast, of course she did. She'd always been the fastest runner in her class. But she'd never seriously thought about running as a sport.

She stood up and pulled on some joggers and her old trainers. She remembered watching the runners training the previous afternoon. It had looked pretty cool. Why not? she said to herself again, and she jogged down the curving stairs and out into the open air.

'Terrific!' said John, when she arrived at the track. 'I'm going to do some stretches before I start. I guess they'll be pretty much the same as what you do in the gym.'

Maxine followed John through a series of warm-ups. She was impressed in spite of herself.

John was warming up just as thoroughly as if a coach had been there, supervising him. 'Ready?' he said when they'd done. 'Let's go for a run.'

They set off, John jogging easily round the track. Maxine enjoyed the smooth springiness under her feet. 'I've never run on a proper track before,' she said.

'I love it,' replied John. 'I'd rather be here, doing this, than just about anywhere else. I can't think of anything better.'

'Have you been doing it for long?' Maxine asked curiously.

'I started when I was seven. My pa took me to football training one night and there was a running track right next door to where we were practising. I'd seen an old video of Michael Johnson running the four hundred metres at the Atlanta Olympics way back in 1996. He was amazing. When I saw that running track I told my pa that I wanted to do it. He took me along the week after. He thought I'd try it out and get bored pretty fast, I guess. But I didn't. Did you know that Michael Johnson is the only athlete ever to have won gold for both the two hundred and the four hundred at the same Olympics?'

'How many times are we going to run round here?' asked Maxine, smiling at John's enthusiasm.

'Oh, about four, I guess. We'll go a little faster next time around.'

'And is that all it is? Just running round and round?'

'I guess. Why? Aren't you having a good time?'

Maxine grinned. 'It's OK.'

John started to pull away from her and she realized that he had increased the pace, though he was still running with exactly the same smooth, relaxed style. They ran three more laps and Maxine soon found that she had no breath to spare for talking. John finally came to a halt at the side of the track and they both stood for a moment, recovering.

'That was fun,' Maxine said, walking across to a bench beside the track and picking up her top. 'I'll see you in the morning. Thanks.'

'Are you kidding?' John replied. 'I was just getting warmed up. I'm going to get down to some real work now. Why don't you sit and watch if you're feeling tired.'

'Huh!' Maxine threw her top back onto the bench and took a swig from her water bottle. 'You have got to be kidding! I want to do whatever you're going to do. Just you try and stop me.'

CHAPTER
SIX

John laughed. 'OK, then,' he said. 'Let's get started.'

He jogged off down the track and Maxine hastily followed him. John's watch beeped once and he picked up speed quickly until the watch beeped again and he settled back into a fast but easy jog. After a few more seconds he glanced across at Maxine, pressed his watch again and sprinted away. It felt to Maxine as though this was faster than the time before, and when she asked John he confirmed it.

'I'm aiming to get up to about seventy-five per cent of my top speed,' he told her. 'Then I slow back down until my heart and my breathing are about back to normal.'

'Is that why you keep looking at me?' she asked him, a little testily. 'You're making sure I'm OK.'

John nodded. 'You shouldn't overdo it,' he said. 'You could injure yourself, trying to keep up.'

'I'll be fine. I'm not an idiot. If it's too hard, then I'll stop.'

'Yeah? Well, don't blame me if you hurt yourself. I am serious, you know.'

Maxine looked at John, running easily beside her, and realized that this wasn't some stupid dare with her friends. It was different. 'Sorry,' she said. 'But I'm still going to try and keep up.'

There was a beep from John's watch, and no more time for talking. Each sprint was just a little faster than the one before, and each recovery time a little longer, but when they stopped for a break a few minutes later, John looked at Maxine in frank astonishment. 'You're not breathing any harder than I am,' he said. 'I honestly thought you'd have to drop out. I don't get it. How come you're so fit?'

'I guess I run around a lot. I do a lot of sport.' Maxine thought for a moment, then started to tick off the sports she did on her fingers. 'There's gymnastics. I do that mostly at school, and in the after-school club. Then there's netball. I'm in a team at the Community Centre, and we have training on Wednesday nights. On Thursdays I have soccer training, and then we usually have a match on Sunday mornings. Plus I go to a street dance class on Mondays.'

'Wow! That's a lot. I only go training three

nights a week, and I still don't have time to get my homework done.'

'Yeah,' said Maxine, with a rueful grin. 'I know what you mean. Homework is a bad thing.'

'Except when it's this kind of homework,' said John. 'I don't mind how much running I do. I figured I'd run a four hundred now. How about it? You want to see how fast you can go?'

'Sure,' said Maxine. 'Are you going to go flat out?'

'I guess so. Look, you can start here, on the inside lane, and I'll start in lane two, down here.'

'That's not fair. It's like, ten metres further on. You'll have a head start.'

'No, I won't. And it's not ten metres either. It's just over seven. If we both started where you are, then the one in the outside lane would have to run further.'

'Well, OK. But why can't I go on the outside?'

'You can if you like. In a race it's easier to be

on the inside, though. You can judge how fast everyone else is going and adjust your pace.'

'Right, then. I'm going on the outside. When I beat you, I don't want you saying it was because I had the best lane.'

John laughed. 'You ain't gonna beat me. Have you ever run a four hundred before? You got no chance. But I'll time you, and we'll find out how fast you really are. I'll say, on your marks, set, and then go.'

Maxine walked forward to the line. She looked back at John. He nodded, and she fixed her attention on the track ahead of her. The sun had dipped behind the trees now, and there was a slight chill in the evening air. She could hear the distant sound of waves breaking on the beach. 'On your marks,' said John. 'Set. GO!'

Maxine took off at top speed, determined not to see John coming past her on the inside. She could hear him, a few paces behind her, as she rounded the top of the first bend and headed into the back straight.

She felt good. She was running faster than she'd run in any of the training sprints, she was sure of that. And she was almost sure that she was gaining on John. She was breathing hard, but that was OK. Her legs felt fine.

She reached the end of the straight and pushed on into the bend. She glanced back over her shoulder and had a quick glimpse of John, still running smoothly, still about the same distance behind her. Suddenly the finish line looked very far away. She tried to accelerate, but she could feel the muscles in her legs starting to burn and she was struggling to get enough air into her lungs.

They were on the final straight now, with just a hundred metres to go. They were the longest hundred metres Maxine had ever run. Somewhere on the straight she saw John streak past her, but she no longer cared about that. Her only thought was to force herself forward over the finish line, but she felt as if she were running through treacle. The last few steps were agony, and as she crossed the line she threw herself to the ground, gasping for air.

After a moment or two she got to her knees and pulled herself upright. 'You were right,' she said with a grimace. 'You're too fast for me.'

John didn't reply at first. He was checking the time on his watch. 'Maybe it's not working properly,' he said finally.

'What do you mean?'

'Your time. It can't be right. You did it in sixty-three seconds!'

'I know I was slow. I mean, I was almost walking at the end, but my legs just wouldn't work.'

'Slow? You weren't slow. You were amazingly fast! I mean, I don't know anything about girls' times, but they have standards for boys and you can bet that you'd beat most boys your age with a time like that.'

'You're serious? I was fast?'

'You bet.'

'But . . . but . . . you beat me easily.'

'Sure I did. I'm a boy, and boys can run faster than girls. You can't do anything about that. Trust me — that was a fast time.'

Maxine shivered suddenly. 'You're getting cold,' said John. 'Put your hoodie on. We'd better jog around the track one more time and then stretch a little.'

'I don't think I can,' said Maxine, pulling on her top.

'You have to,' replied John. 'Stretching afterwards is even more important than stretching before. Come on.'

Maxine forced herself to move her heavy legs slowly around the track. 'Sixty-three seconds?'

she said as they came back around the final bend and she remembered how her legs had stopped working. 'Do you think I could go faster?'

John laughed. 'You bet. For a start, most of the running you do in basketball and soccer is sprinting. You sprint short distances and rest, right?'

Maxine nodded agreement as they reached the end of the track and John started on a series of stretches. 'Well, you probably need to do more long-distance running,' he continued. 'And then there are drills to build up your sprinting ability. You've never done any training for running and you can go as fast as that! With a bit of work you could do anything! You should ask if you can switch to running.'

'I don't know.'

'Well, why not?'

'I'd have to go and see Michael and tell him I want to change – and Isabel too. You know how

Michael goes on about commitment. He's going to hate it if I say I want to change sports after two days.'

'I don't think so. Anyone could see it when you ran across that field. You're a natural.'

They were walking back up the slope towards the main building. Behind them the remnants of a glorious sunset stretched across the sky, but Maxine hardly noticed. The strangest thing was happening inside her. The last hundred metres of the run she had just finished had been total agony, but she wanted to do it again. As soon as possible. She was never going to forget her time. Sixty-three seconds. But she was going to run faster than that. She knew that she could do it.

'Well?' asked John, pausing in the entrance hall before heading off to his room. 'Have you decided?'

'I think so. I'm going to talk to Kayle, but I think I'll go and see Michael in the morning.'

'Cool,' said John. 'Good night, then. And maybe see you down at the track tomorrow.'

He raised a hand and disappeared through the double doors. Maxine walked thoughtfully up the stairs and along the corridor to Kayle's room. Kayle and Sasha were sitting on Kayle's bed looking at a magazine while music played from Kayle's iPod. They both looked up, laughing, when Maxine came in. 'You missed an awesome movie,' Kayle said. 'It's his best yet.'

'He is very handsome,' said Sasha. 'Here, take a look. I am going to bed.'

She handed Maxine the magazine, open at a full-page photograph of Jake Carson, and moved past her to the door. 'How was the running?' she asked. 'You are very crazy not to watch this movie.'

'It was good. I think . . . I think maybe I want to be a runner.'

Sasha's green eyes inspected her seriously.

'Perhaps this is why you are here at Camp Gold,' she said. 'This is fate. It is like a story! If you had not saved me from the bull, you would never have found out your true purpose in life.'

She left suddenly, leaving Kayle and Maxine speechless. Then they both burst out laughing. 'She's amazing,' said Kayle. 'I've never met anyone like her. But you're not serious? You're not really thinking of giving up gymnastics?'

'I'm going to see Michael in the morning. I love it, Kayle. And I'm good at it too. John says I could run even faster.'

Kayle stared at her and Maxine felt herself blushing.

'No,' she said. 'You've got it all wrong.'

'That's what this is really about, isn't it?' said Kayle. 'Admit it, you like him.'

'Well, of course I do,' Maxine began. 'You do too, don't you?' She stopped. 'Oh,' she said, finally understanding. 'You mean you *really* like him?'

'It's not that.' Kayle turned away. 'I thought we were going to do this together,' she mumbled. 'It won't be any fun if you aren't there.'

'I'm sorry. But you know I'll never be as good as you at gymnastics. I want to be a runner. I've decided.'

'Yeah, right. After running round a track a couple of times.' Kayle was suddenly angry. 'Get real, Maxine. Ever since you got here it's like, one minute you're all excited and the next you're in a really bad mood. You never really wanted to come at all, did you?'

'I . . .'

'But now John says he thinks you're a good runner and everything's different. Well, OK then. Go and tell Michael that's what you want to do. See if I care.'

'I thought you'd understand. Sasha does.'

'Well, I don't. OK?'

Maxine felt tears come into her eyes. It was so

unfair. She knew what was upsetting Kayle, but she couldn't help that. She had made up her mind.

She wiped the tears away. 'I don't care what you say,' she told Kayle. 'I'm going to ask Michael if I can switch to running. And I'm going to do it as soon as I possibly can.'

CHAPTER SEVEN

The next morning Maxine was woken by the sun shining in through her window. For a moment she didn't know where she was, but she knew that she had something very important to do.

Then she remembered. She had to go and see Michael, and she had to do it as soon as possible. She looked at the clock on her bedside table and saw that it was only seven-thirty. Breakfast at

Camp Gold didn't start until eight, but maybe Michael would be up already. There was no point sitting in her room.

She showered and dressed quickly, then made her way downstairs. There was nobody about as she pushed through the glass door of the corridor where all the offices were located. The place was completely empty, and she was about to leave when she saw Michael's name on a door.

MICHAEL GLADSTONE. PRINCIPAL.

She might as well give it a try. With her heart beating fast, she stepped forward and knocked, very quietly.

There was no one there. Why would there be at this time in the morning? She was already turning away when she heard a deep voice say, 'Isabel? Is that you?'

She tried to speak, but the words stuck in her throat. She coughed. 'Er . . . it's not Isabel. It's

Maxine.' Her voice sounded squeaky. She felt like running away. But then the door opened and Michael stood there, towering above her.

'Maxine? What can I do for you? You're up very early.'

'I know. I couldn't sleep. I wanted to ask you . . . Could I . . . Do you think I'd be able to change to athletics?'

Michael smiled suddenly. 'I think you'd better come in,' he said. 'Take a seat.' He hastily removed a pile of folders from a chair. 'It gets a little untidy in here,' he said apologetically. 'I don't really think I'm cut out for office work.'

Maxine was staring at Michael's desk. It was almost invisible beneath teetering piles of books and papers.

'Now then,' he said, sitting down behind the desk and resting his chin on his hand. 'You want to change sports. What's brought this on? Not being chased by a bull?'

'That was stupid,' Maxine said. 'I mean, we didn't know there was a bull, or we wouldn't have—'

'It's OK,' said Michael, laughing. 'The bull wouldn't have hurt you. Not unless he'd fallen over on top of you. He's out with the herd, is very old and his fighting days are over. But anyway, why have you changed your mind?'

'I went running last night,' Maxine said. 'I went with John. We did everything properly. Warmed up and everything. And I loved it. I . . .'

'Yes?'

Maxine was about to tell Michael about her time, about how fast she had run, but she felt suddenly self-conscious. 'We . . . we ran a four hundred metres. John says . . . well, he says I ran fast. He says it was a good time.'

'OK.' Maxine saw a twinkle in Michael's eye

and instantly felt better. 'Tell me, then,' he said. 'What time did you do?'

Maxine told him.

'I'm sorry?' Michael had been reaching for a pen, but he stopped, his hand hovering in mid-air. 'What did you say?'

'Sixty-three seconds.'

'Well, you know what? That is very fast. I thought you looked like a runner. And you haven't been enjoying the gymnastics, have you?'

'I have been trying, though,' Maxine said. 'I did my best.'

'I know. Isabel told me. I think we'd better talk to her, and also to Greg. He's the running coach. Let's go and find them.'

'You mean, I can do it?'

'It depends if Greg has room for you,' said Michael, standing up. 'We allocated the Camp Gold places carefully, you see. Ten sprinters. Ten distance runners. You get the idea.'

'Oh.' Maxine felt suddenly deflated. She had assumed that all she had to do was persuade Michael.

Then the door opened and she heard Isabel's voice. 'Good morning, Michael. Are you ready yet? I—' She stopped when she saw Maxine, and flashed a quick, enquiring glance at Michael. He gave a very slight shake of his head.

'It's good that you came by, Isabel,' he said. 'Maxine came to ask me about the possibility of changing to athletics. Running, to be exact. What do you think?'

'Well, if you're serious about changing, then I think it's a shame!' Isabel exclaimed, to Maxine's surprise. 'I think you could be a terrific gymnast, Maxine,' she said. 'You work hard. I've been very impressed. I like people who persist.'

Maxine felt the colour rising to her face. She hadn't expected this. She found herself explaining again what had happened the previous evening when she had trained with John.

'To run a time like that,' Michael said, 'with no real training, that really is raw talent. It's what Camp Gold is all about, right? Finding raw talent and turning it into pure gold.'

'You need to be sure,' Isabel said, looking directly into Maxine's eyes.

Maxine held her gaze. 'I am,' she said. 'This is what I want to do.'

'Right, then,' said Isabel, suddenly business-like. 'Let's find Greg and see what he says.'

As they emerged from the office corridor Maxine saw Sasha and Kayle coming towards them, heading for breakfast. Kayle saw her and looked away, but Sasha's eyes were shining and she gave Maxine a quick thumbs-up sign as she walked past.

The running coach was already down at the track, dragging small hurdles into position. He saw them approaching and stood up, looking curiously at Maxine. Michael quickly explained the situation.

'Is this OK with you?' Greg asked Isabel.

'If it's really what Maxine wants, I think we should let her do it,' Isabel said.

'There are a couple of problems,' Greg said. 'First, girls your age don't usually run four hundreds. We'll need to figure out whether you're a sprinter or a distance runner. What do you think?'

'I don't know,' Maxine replied, feeling foolish. John should have told her girls didn't run four hundreds. 'A sprinter, maybe,' she said, thinking how they'd talked last night about how most of the running she'd done was sprinting.

'OK,' said Greg, nodding his head. 'We can give it a try. You can obviously run fast. How about running gear? Have you got any?'

Maxine shook her head glumly. That was

another thing she hadn't considered.

Greg smiled suddenly. 'Don't look so worried. Camp Gold is sponsored by sportswear manufacturers, in case you hadn't noticed. We have dozens of pairs of running shoes. Let's get you sorted out. And then we'd better have breakfast or those young gannets will have eaten it all!'

In the restaurant Maxine found John, Sasha and Kayle all sitting at their usual table. They had finished eating and John and Sasha looked up expectantly when Maxine came over with her tray. Kayle looked down at her plate.

'What did they say?' asked John.

'It's OK,' Maxine told them. 'I can do it. Greg even gave me a pair of running shoes. I can't quite believe it.'

'Very good,' said Sasha. 'I told you, Kayle. I knew they would think it was good idea.'

Kayle pushed back her chair. 'I have to go and

get ready,' she said, still without looking at Maxine. 'I'll see you later.'

Maxine felt terrible. Kayle was her oldest friend and she hated falling out with her. But she was excited at the same time, and she felt a huge relief at not having to endure another session in the gym. Besides, she told herself, she had fallen out with Kayle plenty of times before, and they had always been cool. Kayle just needed time, that was all.

After breakfast she went to her room and called home. 'I've sorted everything out, Mum,' she said, when her mother answered the phone. 'I'm not doing gymnastics any more. I'm going to be a runner.' There was a long pause at the other end of the phone. 'Mum? Are you still there?'

'I just hope you're doing the right thing,' her mum said finally.

'I am. I know I am.'

'It's just . . . you do kind of flit about from one thing to another, Maxine. Don't you think you ought to stick to one thing?'

'I will, Mum. I promise. This is it, really it is.'

'Well, if you're sure. You don't want to come home, then?'

Maxine realized with a shock that it was only the previous afternoon when she had been planning to run away. 'No, Mum, everything's fine. I'll call you later.'

She put her new running shoes in her bag and went to meet John and Sasha outside. They walked down to the track together, and Maxine felt as if everyone was looking at her. They left Sasha with the small group of pole-vaulters and she and John walked over to join the runners. Now everyone was definitely staring at her, and with a sinking heart she realized that Tamsin's two friends were there, flashing her unfriendly looks.

'This is Maxine, everyone,' said Greg, introducing her. 'We think she might be a sprinter, so she's going to work with you guys today.'

He told her the names of all the other runners. Tamsin's friends were called Oliver and Melissa, and she soon discovered that they were sprinters too. When they had finished warming up Greg took the sprinters over to the infield where he had marked out a large square with cones. 'We'll start with Shadow Run,' he said. 'John, you and Maxine can shadow each other. Show her what to do.'

'It's easy,' John said as they waited for Greg's whistle. 'You try and stay right behind me, and I try to lose you. Watch out for everyone else though. We change over every time the whistle goes.'

Maxine loved the game. She found it easy to dodge in and out of the other runners, and she tagged John every time she was chasing. When it was his turn, he never caught her once. 'This is easy,' she said, laughing, as Greg blew his whistle for the final time. 'Is it all like this?'

'It gets harder,' replied John. 'Don't worry about that.'

Forty-five minutes later Maxine sat on the grass with the others wondering how she could ever have thought it was easy. Most of the activities they had done had been games, but with every game they had played the demands had got tougher.

'OK,' said Greg. 'We'll do a loop of rolling sprints, and then some timed races to finish. Two teams of five. John can explain it to you,' he said to Maxine.

'When Greg whistles, the one at the back sprints to the front,' John said hurriedly. 'Then when he whistles again, the next one goes. It's harder than it looks.'

'Like everything else,' Maxine said.

'But you're enjoying it, right?' asked John.

Maxine grinned. 'Of course I am. Hey, get ready, we're starting.'

They set off. The leader was a small, dark-haired girl called Grace. Maxine was next, then John. Melissa was behind him and another boy brought up the rear. There was a blast from Greg's whistle and the boy sprinted to the front and settled down in the lead. After a few seconds the whistle blew again, and Melissa moved forward. As she passed Maxine she brushed against her elbow.

'Oi! Watch what you're doing,' she yelled over her shoulder.

'I hardly touched her,' Maxine said to John behind her, but there was no reply. Greg's whistle had blown again, and now it was John racing to the front. Me next, thought Maxine, waiting for the whistle. When it came she put her head down and ran as fast as she knew how, but as she passed Melissa she felt a sharp pain on her leg and staggered sideways, struggling to stay upright.

At first she was too stunned to react. Melissa had kicked her! But no one else seemed to have noticed. 'That's it, Maxine,' called Greg. 'Stay on your feet. Well done!'

She reached the front and slowed down. The final runner came up to the front and Greg called all the runners together. 'We'll have some races now,' he said. 'Boys first. Sixty-metre sprint.'

Oliver won by a clear metre, with Melissa applauding loudly. Then it was the girls' turn. Maxine crouched at the start and saw Melissa lining up beside her. She heard her whisper, fast and low. 'You were no good at gym,' she hissed. 'And you'll be rubbish at this. You may as well give up now.'

CHAPTER EIGHT

'On your marks . . . set . . . GO!'

Maxine wasn't ready. She was a fraction of a second slower than any of the other girls to react to the command, and that fraction of a second transformed itself at once into a gap of nearly a metre between herself and the rest. Melissa had put her off, and Maxine was annoyed with herself for listening to her. She knew she should have shut her annoying chatter out of her mind.

Even as all these thoughts flashed through Maxine's head she was driving herself forward, accelerating with every pace she took, and now she was definitely catching them! She went past the back marker easily and the rest of the runners were neck and neck, only thirty centimetres ahead of her. Another two strides and she was clear.

She heard a grunt of astonishment from Melissa on her left, and now the finish was coming up fast. She drove for the line, pushing her legs as hard as they would go. There were fifteen metres left . . . Ten . . .

She was going to do it.

And then suddenly she wasn't moving so fast. Her brain was sending messages to her legs. Faster. Push. Come on! But nothing was happening. She was slowing up and there was nothing she could do to stop it happening. With two metres left to run, the other competitors flashed past her. Every one of them.

She was last.

'Hey, Maxine, that was good. You nearly made it.' John crouched next to her where she'd flopped down, gasping air into her lungs.

'I lost. I was last.'

'Big deal. It was your first race and you don't even know if you're going to be a sprinter yet. The main thing is, you were fast. If you hadn't had such a terrible start you would have won.'

Maxine looked up. 'You think so? Really?'

'He's right, you know.' Greg had come up behind them while they were talking. The other girls were all chatting together in a big group, but Maxine saw Melissa's eyes flicking over towards her and John. Greg reached down with a strong sun-tanned arm and pulled her to her feet. 'For a first race that was solid. These girls have been sprinting for a couple of years, most of them. And if we teach you how to start better, I think you'll be more than a match for them. See you the day after tomorrow!'

'What did he mean?' Maxine asked as Greg walked away and they started back.

'You've forgotten, haven't you?' laughed John. 'Tomorrow is a rest day. No training. No classes. We could all do something together – me, you, Sasha and Kayle.'

'Kayle's mad at me,' Maxine said, still glowing inside from Greg's comments. 'She thinks I should have stuck with gymnastics. We've always done it together.'

'I could see. But you two are old friends, right? You wouldn't fall out over something like this?'

'I hope not. Oh no! Not again.'

They were nearing the pole-vault pit, and Sasha had just hit the landing pad in an ungainly mixture of elbows, ankles, pole and bar. She jumped to her feet, laughing. 'That time I was very close,' she told them when she noticed them watching her anxiously. They all stood and craned their necks upwards as two assistants lifted the bar back onto its supports. 'If I can get over this it will be personal best. I think I do it next time.'

'She must be totally fearless,' Maxine said to John as they sat down on a grassy bank to watch. 'That bar is almost as high as a house.'

At the far end of the runway Sasha was going through her preparation routine. 'Did Melissa say something to you?' John asked suddenly. 'It looked like she was trying to put you off at the start of the race.'

'It was nothing. I won't let her do it again. It's what Greg says that counts, right?'

'Right. Only I kind of feel responsible. I got us off to a bad start with those three.'

'You? It was them,' Maxine said indignantly. 'They had it in for us right from the beginning.'

'I guess,' said John a little doubtfully. 'It's just a shame we can't be friends with them. Oliver's a great four hundred runner. He works real hard, and when he's not with the girls he's kind of cool.'

'Huh! If you think I'll ever be friends with Melissa and Tamsin you are totally crazy. Look. Here goes Sasha.'

The tall Russian girl was racing towards them with her pole held out in front. She slammed it into the box and rose into the air like a bird. 'Wow!' breathed John. 'That is just awesome!'

Sasha's feet curved up and over the bar as she pushed upwards with her arms and let the pole fall away. 'She's going to do it!' yelled Maxine. 'Oh, no!'

As Sasha's long, thin body curled over the bar the hem of her shorts touched it. It was just the faintest of grazes, but the bar wobbled, vibrating along its length, and as Sasha hit the pad it tumbled down on top of her. She looked at it for a second in disbelief, then shook her head and stood up, laughing. 'I guess I will have to wait till tomorrow.'

'The day after that,' said Maxine. 'Tomorrow we're going to have fun.'

The following day Maxine woke late. She jumped out of bed in a panic, thinking that she would have missed breakfast and be late for training. Then she remembered that today there was a late breakfast, and after that the day was theirs to use however they liked. She made her way to the restaurant determined to apologize to Kayle, only to find her friend waiting for her in the entrance hall, sitting on one of the large leather sofas. Kayle jumped up when she saw Maxine.

'Hey, Maxine, I'm sorry. I've been a pig. I know you never liked gymnastics that much. And

John says he thinks you might be the top runner out of all the girls. I've got to admit, that's kind of cool.'

Maxine gave Kayle a hug. 'Yeah, well, I'm sorry too,' she said. 'It's just so exciting. I mean, it's not just that I can run fast. I really, really like it. And I've got to admit, I'm not going to miss those ballet classes one little bit!'

'Yeah, the ballet is hard. But now we're having street dance classes too. We had the first one yesterday.'

For a second, Maxine felt a pang of jealousy. She loved street dance. And she was good at it. It would have been nice not to be the worst person in the gym class for a change. Then she shrugged. 'Oh, well,' she said. 'I guess I can't do everything.'

'No,' said Kayle. 'Only I was wondering. Maybe you could help me with some moves?'

'Oh, right,' said Maxine with a grin. 'So that was why you wanted to make up?'

'No, I . . . Well, yeah, a bit, obviously. So you'll help me?'

'Sure.' Maxine held out a hand and Kayle slapped it. 'We'll make sure you have the best moves of anyone. Let's get breakfast. The others are planning to go swimming this morning. What do you think? I haven't even seen the indoor pool properly yet. It's meant to be fantastic.'

Over breakfast Maxine told Kayle everything that had happened to her the day before. 'I want to see these new running shoes,' Kayle said. 'Maybe I should change to running myself if you get gear like that. Can I have your room card and I'll go check them out! We're the same size so I could try them on.'

'Oh, the room's not locked,' Maxine said. 'The card kept getting stuck.'

'We'll see you outside then,' John said. 'In the usual place. Under the tree.'

Kayle ran off ahead of Maxine, jumping up

the stairs three at a time. 'I'm glad you made friends again,' Sasha said seriously. 'Kayle is very happy now, I think.'

'Me too,' said Maxine. 'See you in a minute.'

She followed Kayle up the stairs, and just as she entered the corridor leading to her room she heard a crash and a scream. 'Kayle?' she yelled. 'Was that you?'

She raced down the corridor to her room. The door was open, and at first she could make no sense of the scene that met her eyes. The air was filled with a drifting white cloud, and a film of pale dust had settled over everything. There were splashes of yellow on the carpet and on Kayle's back, where she was sitting on the floor clutching her head. She looked like a ghost, but for the splash of brilliant red seeping from a small cut on her forehead. She looked up at Maxine.

'It was a booby trap, look.' She indicated a metal wastepaper bin that was lying on the carpet. 'It must have been on top of the door. It was full of flour and eggs. Look at this mess!'

'But your head. Are you OK?'

'It's nothing. Just a little cut. You know who did this, don't you?'

'I can guess. We'd never prove it, though.'

'So, what do you think? Should we tell someone?'

Maxine thought for a moment. 'You know what?' she said finally. 'I bet it would annoy them a whole lot more if we pretended it never happened.'

'Yeah? How are we going to do that? We'll never be able to clean all this up.'

Maxine walked quickly to the end of the corridor and stopped outside a door marked STAFF ONLY. She checked both ways, then opened the door and grabbed a bucket of cleaning materials. Then she dragged the vacuum cleaner along to her room.

She fastened a little brush to the end of the vacuum cleaner tube and started sucking the flour from Kayle's clothes and hair. 'Better,' she said at last. 'You look a bit less like a ghost now. But maybe you should take a shower.'

The vacuum cleaner hadn't managed to remove all the flour. Kayle's face was pale and her hair was streaked with white and matted with egg and bits of shell. A dribble of fresh blood had run down above one eye. Suddenly Maxine couldn't contain her laughter any longer. 'You do look kind of weird,' she said. 'Take a look in the mirror.'

Kayle went into the bathroom. Maxine was worried for a moment that she might have upset her, and she was relieved when Kayle burst out laughing. She came back into the room with her eyes staring and her hands stretched out ahead of her. 'I'm a zombie!' she croaked. 'I'm undead.'

'Go on,' Maxine said, backing away. 'Get in the

shower. I'll get you some clean clothes and I'll finish cleaning this up.' She laughed. 'It's no worse than helping Mum clean up at home after Joshua's had some mates over!'

When Kayle emerged from the shower a few minutes later she stood and stared in astonishment. Apart for a few damp patches on the carpet, the room looked perfect. 'OK?' said Maxine. 'No one will ever know. We pretend it didn't happen, right? And we can start thinking of a way to get back at them.'

When they told John and Sasha what had happened they were outraged. 'We could play the same trick on one of them,' suggested Sasha.

'No good,' said Maxine. 'They'll be expecting that. There's no chance they'll leave their doors open.'

'What about eggs in the end of their shoes?' said Kayle. 'Imagine what that would feel like.'

'Or if we could get chilli powder on their

food somehow,' said John. 'I'd love to see their faces.'

They started walking towards the swimming pool, talking excitedly as they went.

Maxine had the feeling that Tamsin and her friends were going to regret that they had started this war!

CHAPTER NINE

The swimming pool was on a part of the site they hadn't thoroughly explored, and none of them had been inside it before. So when they entered the pool area from the changing rooms they simply stood there, staring in amazement.

'I've never seen a pool this big,' said Maxine.

'I have,' said John, 'but only on TV. Look, there's even a diving pool.'

As he spoke Maxine saw Tamsin standing on

the top diving platform. She stood very still for a moment, then took off. She seemed to be in the air for a very long time before plunging into the water with the smallest of splashes. There was a pause, and then she burst up from the water, punching the air with one hand. She swam to the side of the pool, cutting through the water like a seal, and pulled herself out to join her friends and exchange high fives with them.

'You know what?' said Maxine. 'That was seriously cool. It's a shame she has to be our enemy.'

'Well, she is,' replied Kayle. 'And if you think I'm going to forget about that booby trap just because she can dive off the top platform then you are crazy.'

'Come on,' said John. 'Let's race. Two lengths of the pool, OK. Ready? Go.'

John was already airborne. 'Cheat!' yelled Maxine before diving in after him and launching into a fast, even, front-crawl stroke. She glanced over and saw Kayle moving smoothly beside her. John was a couple of metres clear of them and Sasha was nowhere to be seen. Kayle and Maxine kept up with John until he made a smooth racing turn at the far end of the pool. As the girls turned Maxine saw that he had gained further on them, and she also saw Sasha labouring towards them with a clumsy breast-stroke. Maxine set off in pursuit of John, but it was hopeless, and he was already sitting on the side of the pool when she finished, half a metre ahead of Kayle.

'You're an expert,' Maxine gasped, accusingly. 'You didn't say.'

'I bet you're in your school swimming team,' said Kayle, shaking the water from her hair.

'Yeah, well,' replied John, looking a little embarrassed. 'I did swim in the regional championships last year.'

'I bet he won too,' said Maxine.

'Did you?' demanded Kayle.

'Well, yes.' This time John was definitely blushing.

'OK,' said Maxine as Sasha finally finished her two lengths. 'This time you can give us a head start. And then we'd better teach Sasha how to swim properly.'

'That would be good,' said Sasha. 'Then I can go fast like all of you. At the moment I am like a snail.'

They spent half an hour showing Sasha how to swim front-crawl. 'You learn fast,' Maxine told her when she had managed to swim a width of the pool, breathing comfortably on both sides.

'I have good teachers, I think,' Sasha said. 'Hey, look, we have things to play with.'

Two of the coaches were launching a large inflatable raft onto the water and throwing in a selection of floats, balls and inflatables. They all swam to the raft, and it seemed that everyone in the pool had the same idea. Maxine hauled herself out of the water and stood up a little unsteadily on the slippery surface. The others scrambled up beside her and Sasha grabbed hold of Maxine's arm with a little scream. 'It is very wobbly, I think,' she said.

'OK, everyone,' yelled John over the noise. 'Let's all jump together, OK? One—'

But before John could finish counting Maxine felt someone shove her hard from behind. She was taken completely by surprise and catapulted into the water with an enormous splash. Her nose and goggles filled with water and she came to the surface choking and very angry. 'How could you?' she yelled at the others, who were treading water beside her. 'You—'

She stopped. A short distance away she saw Melissa and Tamsin laughing together as they swam away.

'You know what,' Maxine said to the others. 'I can't believe I almost thought she was cool. We are going to have to do something about them. And soon.'

The next morning Maxine made her way down to the track with John and Sasha. She had spent two hours with Kayle and Sasha the night before working on some body-popping ideas for Kayle's floor routine. They had spent half the time laughing at Sasha's hopeless attempts to copy what they were doing, but she was the same with dancing as she was with pole-vaulting and swimming. She absolutely refused to give up – no matter how crazy she looked.

Maxine grinned at her now, and Sasha laughed. 'I practised my moves this morning,' she said, as if she'd been reading Maxine's mind. 'I think I am beginning to get the hang of it.'

They had arrived at the track, where Greg and

the other coaches were waiting for them. 'It's another fine morning,' Greg said, gathering all the athletes around him. 'So we're all going for a run on the beach. Pole-vaulters and javelin throwers too, all of us! Is everyone here? Let's go.'

He set off down the path to the little gate in the wall, moving at a gentle jog. Once through the gate he speeded up a little as they followed the path past the field with the cows and zigzagged down through the dunes to the sea.

'Take off your shoes if you like,' Greg said, jogging out onto the beach. The tide was out and there was a wide strip of flat, shining wet sand. 'We'll be coming back the same way.'

They all removed their trainers and raced down to the edge of the sea. Maxine ran into the waves, shouting like the others at the delicious coldness. Soon everyone was in the water up to their knees, jumping about and splashing each other. 'Enough,' called Greg at last. 'We're going to run two kilometres that way, and then back again. For the runners, I'll set the pace so you can aim to keep up, but we *all* need to build our stamina, even you field sports guys, so everyone do the best you can.'

He set off along the hard sand. Maxine ran with Sasha and John, splashing in the gentle ripples at the very edge of the water. As they ran, the line of runners gradually began to stretch out behind them, and before long Sasha dropped back, leaving Maxine and John running beside a slim, dark-haired girl.

The strip of sand between the cliffs and the sea was becoming narrower now, and they were approaching a rocky promontory that marked the end of the bay. When they reached it, Greg paused for a few moments to let all the runners catch up. Maxine saw that many of them – especially the non-runners – were red-faced and breathing hard. She was surprised, because she was having no trouble keeping up with Greg. In fact, she felt as if she could run faster.

Greg set off again, and this time only Maxine and the small, dark-haired girl kept up with him. Even John had fallen behind. The girl looked across at Maxine as they ran, and Maxine smiled, but the girl looked away again quickly. As they approached the place they had started from Maxine felt Greg increase the pace once more, but she was able to match him easily. She felt as if she could run for ever, and she was disappointed when they stopped to let the others catch up again.

She waded a short distance into the sea, then bent and splashed water over her head. She turned and saw Greg watching her. 'You see?' he said. 'I thought you might be a distance runner. A lot of these sprinters found that hard, but you didn't, did you?'

Maxine shook her head. 'It was fun.'

'I think you should try the eight hundred metres. Like Jade here.' He indicated the slim girl with a nod of his head. Jade looked at Maxine appraisingly, then turned away and walked back up the beach to put on her trainers. 'She's a good runner,' Greg said, laughing. 'You'll have your work cut out if you're going to compete with her.'

Jade ran off up the path towards Camp Gold, tossing a final look over her shoulder. John and Sasha walked over to join Maxine in the water.

'What did Greg say?' asked John. 'I couldn't keep up with you.'

'He thinks I should run the eight hundred metres. That's her distance.' Maxine pointed at the slim girl disappearing up the path. 'She's called Jade. I don't think she likes me much.'

'She does not even know you,' Sasha said. 'That is foolish.'

'Maybe,' replied Maxine. 'But it's true.'

The rest of the training session was uneventful. Maxine moved on to train with the small group of distance runners. Their coach was a tall, wiry Australian runner called Kath. Her skin was dark golden brown from the Australian sun and Maxine instantly liked her a lot. Jade ignored Maxine completely while they worked, but that was fine. Maxine was just pleased to get away from Melissa's annoying comments and dirty looks. At the end of the session Kath called them together. 'We'll be having a race day tomorrow,' she told them. 'A chance for you to really show us what you can do. No training in the morning. Just a gentle jog if you feel like it. See you here tomorrow afternoon. Hey, Maxine, wait a moment, will you?'

Maxine stayed behind as the others dispersed.

'Look, I know you've never run an eight hundred before,' Kath said, 'but you should still have a go, right? Just to get the feel of what a race is like. I don't want you to be too disappointed, though, if the other girls are faster than you. You're going to be good, Maxine. I can see that. But it won't happen all at once, OK?'

Maxine nodded and went off to join her friends. It had been a great morning, despite Kath's warning about tomorrow. She could still feel some of the elation she'd experienced, running along the beach, tracking Greg's footsteps and feeling as if she could just run and run.

'You look happy, I think,' Sasha said as they walked back afterwards. 'At last you have found what you are meant to do. It is your fate for sure.'

Maxine and John laughed. Sometimes Sasha could be very serious.

'It was good,' agreed Maxine. 'But it's a shame we didn't get to run any races. Now I'm training to run eight hundred metres and I don't even

know if I'm any good at it yet. And I have
to run a race tomorrow. Kath thinks I won't
do that well. It would be good to surprise her.'

'There's an easy way to find out how fast you
are,' said John. 'We'll come back tonight, like we
did before. I'll time you. Then you'll know for
sure.'

'Great,' said Maxine. 'I'll get Kayle to come
too. Hey, watch out!'

Someone dashed between her and Sasha,
forcing both of them off the narrow path. It was
Jade. She didn't look back. They watched her run
up to the entrance and go inside. 'She is a very
strange girl,' Sasha said.

'You can say that again,' agreed Maxine.

She spent the afternoon helping Kayle with her
dance moves. Kayle was excited at the idea of
Maxine being a distance runner. 'Hey,' she said
as Maxine plugged her iPod into the sound

system in the dance studio and the heavy bass of Kayle's chosen track thudded through the floor. 'Maybe you'll run even further. Maybe you'll be a marathon runner.'

Maxine laughed. 'I don't think they let you until you're older,' she said.

'Just forget about that for a second and show me how to do that weird slow-motion thing with your arms. It's really cool and it fits into my routine. Yeah, that one!'

The girls worked on it all afternoon. When they finally stopped Kayle led the way into the main gym and showed Maxine how she planned to transition from a series of tumbles into the moves they'd worked out. 'Genius,' said Maxine. 'It's completely awesome!'

'Good,' said Kayle, pleased. 'The street dance teacher is OK, but she doesn't know stuff like you do. I'll just try it one more time.'

Kayle repeated the sequence, even better than

before, Maxine thought. As she finished, the sound of clapping came from the far end of the gym. The girls turned and saw Michael and Isabel. 'Very nice,' Isabel said. 'I'm looking forward to seeing the whole thing. Keep up the good work, girls.'

With that the two of them made their way outside.

'How long do you think they'd been there?' Kayle asked Maxine when they had gone. 'And what were they doing here anyway?'

'It's nothing. He's helping her with some problem, right?'

'Maybe. But, if you ask me, he looked embarrassed. There's definitely something going on between them.'

CHAPTER TEN

John, Sasha, Maxine and Kayle waited until all the other students had made their way into the evening's movie before setting out for the track. The sun had sunk in the west and there were high bars of pink cloud spreading across the sky as they made their way down the path. Sasha was describing Kayle's gymnastics routine to John, but Maxine was quiet. She was feeling nervous flutters in her stomach, even though this wasn't going to be a race. Except, of course, that it *would* be a race.

A race against herself.

It was only when they reached the track that Maxine noticed that all the others had trainers on their feet, and when she stripped off, ready to warm up, she found that under their loose clothes they were all wearing shorts and T-shirts too. 'We thought we might as well help you to warm up,' Kayle said with a grin. 'You've been helping me, after all.'

'It is fair,' Sasha said. 'Thanks to you I can swim like a very slow fish, and I have excellent dance moves.'

They were all laughing as they stretched their limbs and set off round the track at a gentle jog. 'OK,' said John after a couple of laps. 'Are you ready, Maxine?'

'Sure,' said Maxine, although she didn't feel ready. Her heart was beating fast and she was taking deep breaths to calm herself. If she was like this on her own, what would she be like before the race tomorrow?

'Here,' said John, handing his watch to Sasha. 'You know how this works, don't you?'

'Of course,' Sasha said.

'What are you doing?' asked Maxine.

'I'm going to run the first lap with you,' John said. 'You've never done this before and the chances are you'll go off too fast. Two minutes thirty would be a real good time, I guess, so I'll take you through four hundred in seventy-five seconds. What you do after that is up to you.'

'Can you do that? How will you know how fast you're going?'

'Trust me,' said John, with a nod of the head to Sasha.

'On your marks . . . set . . . GO!' she called.

At the word GO Maxine felt as if she had been electrified. She bolted forward as if she was racing for a bus, but after a few metres she realized that John wasn't with her and she forced herself to slow down. 'That's good,' he said, moving past her on the outside. 'Just fall in behind me and keep up. It's easier if you run behind.'

After that John didn't speak any more. The pace felt comfortable to Maxine, but it still left little breath for talking. They rounded the top bend and headed down the straight, still at the same even pace, and came up to where Kayle and Sasha was waiting. 'Seventy–five seconds dead,' Sasha called out as Maxine passed her.

'Go for it, Maxine,' said John, stepping over the kerb and jogging off onto the grassy field. 'Keep this pace down the back straight and then give it all you've got.'

Maxine heard what John said, but it wasn't that easy. She felt good and this pace felt too slow. She knew she could run faster. She pushed a little harder and she still felt good so she pressed on, faster still. She was running the final bend now, and she could see her friends waiting at the end of the straight. There was no point doing this if she didn't give it all she had. She accelerated again, but now it started to hurt. It hurt in her legs and it hurt in her lungs but she didn't care. She hurtled down the straight and threw herself across the finish line. She jogged a few more paces, then bent double, fighting for breath.

She stood up and saw her three friends all looking at the stopwatch in Sasha's hands. 'What does it mean?' Kayle asked. 'Is it good or not?'

'Of course it's good,' said John. 'Two minutes twenty-one. It's only a few seconds off the National standard.'

There was a sudden noise at the top of the grassy slope that surrounded the track. They all turned and saw a watching figure, silhouetted against the darkening sky. It was Jade. She turned quickly and walked back up the path to the main building.

'Don't worry about her,' said Kayle as they watched her go. 'You did a great time, that's what matters, isn't it?'

'I don't know,' Maxine replied. 'I don't like having enemies. It spoils everything.'

'No, it doesn't,' said Kayle. 'It makes life interesting. What are we going to do to get back at Tamsin and Melissa and Oliver? I've had some interesting ideas.'

'Tell us,' said Maxine. 'I knew you'd think of something.'

Talking excitedly, the four made their way back inside.

When lunch was over the following afternoon John suggested shooting some baskets while they waited for the athletics competition. Kayle went to the gym to practise, but John, Sasha and Maxine dumped their bags by the wall and were soon involved in a neat new game that John showed them. It was Sasha who noticed the time. 'We had better run, I think. The pole-vault starts in fifteen minutes and I have not warmed up yet.'

'We haven't even changed,' said Maxine, grabbing her bag. As she picked it up it slipped out of her hand and fell on the tarmac, spilling her tracksuit. She bundled the things back inside and raced after the others, annoyed with herself for forgetting about the time.

When they reached the track, the other athletes were all spread out around the grassy infield, warming up. Kath saw her coming. 'This is no good, Maxine,' she said. 'Get changed as fast as you can. You should have been here ten minutes ago.'

'I know,' Maxine said. 'I'm sorry.'

'Well, go on then.'

Maxine turned and ran into the changing rooms. She unzipped her bag, pulled out her clothes and stared into the bottom of the bag in horrified astonishment. Her running shoes weren't there!

She scrabbled frantically through the pile of clothes. Nothing. They must have fallen out somehow when she dropped the bag. How could she have failed to notice? She rushed out of the door and raced back up the path, ignoring a shout from Kath.

Back at the basketball court there was no sign of the shoes. She couldn't believe it. She must have left them in her room. She dashed into the building and along the corridor, fumbling with her key card in her haste. She looked under the bed, in the cupboards, everywhere. There were no shoes. Only her muddy old trainers with the trim peeling off them.

From outside came the sounds of cheering as the first events began. Maxine felt like bursting into tears, but she bit her lip and forced herself to think. There was no point wasting more time looking for her running shoes. She had no choice. She would have to run in her old trainers. She picked them up and sprinted back down the corridor.

By the time she made it back to the changing rooms she felt as if she had already run a race. She changed quickly and splashed some water on her face, then stepped outside to find Greg and Kath both waiting for her, grim-faced. 'What's going on, Maxine?' asked Greg. 'And what are those?'

He was looking down at her feet. Maxine felt the blood rushing to her face. 'I couldn't find my running shoes,' she stammered. 'They weren't in my bag and I had to go back to look for them. I'm sorry.'

'You've lost the shoes?' asked Greg. 'I don't believe it. You've only had them a couple of days. This is crazy, Maxine. I really hope you're not wasting our time. You'd better go and prepare for your race. I'm disappointed. I was hoping for great things from you.'

Maxine jogged out onto the grassy field beyond the athletics area. There were tears misting her eyes as she forced herself to go through her warm-up routine. It was so unfair. She simply couldn't understand what had happened to the shoes. She did a couple of circuits of the field, gradually increasing her pace. At least all the running around didn't seem to have slowed her down.

She finished her warm-up and headed back to the track, where she arrived just in time to see John finish second to Oliver in his four-hundred-metre race. He pulled on a sweatshirt and came over to join her, his face shining. 'I did a PB,' he said. 'A personal best! Pretty cool, huh?'

'Yeah, that's amazing. It's a pity it had to be him who beat you, though.' She indicated Oliver with her head. He was deep in conversation with Melissa.

'Well, he may be stuck up, but he's a hell of a runner,' John said. 'My only hope is, I think he's nearly a year older than me, and I haven't finished growing yet. So maybe I'll beat him one day.'

'It can't be soon enough for me.'

'Hey, where have you been anyway?' asked John, looking more closely at Maxine. 'Have you been crying?'

'It's my shoes,' Maxine said miserably. 'I can't find them anywhere. I was sure I put them in my bag, but when I got down here, they were gone. I can't believe I've been so stupid.'

'Maybe you haven't,' said John thoughtfully. 'We weren't really watching the bags when we were playing ball, were we? But I could have sworn your bag was zipped up when we got there. And look over there.'

Maxine followed his gaze and saw Oliver and Melissa watching them. Melissa said something to Oliver, and they both laughed. 'I hate her,' Maxine said. 'That is so mean. I'm going to tell her what I think of her.'

'Don't,' said John, grabbing her arm. 'You need to focus on your race. Having a row isn't going to help anyone now. And besides, you'd miss Sasha. There are only two of them left in the competition and I want to watch.'

'You're right.' Maxine took a deep breath and followed John to their usual vantage point on the grassy slope near the pole-vault landing pit. They arrived just as Sasha's rival, Nabila, ran up for her final jump. She rose like a bird, but scraped the bar with her shoulder as she flew over it. Just for a second it trembled on its supports, before falling to the ground.

Nabila thumped the landing pad with her hand before jumping to her feet. She saw John and Sasha watching and sat down beside them to watch Sasha's final attempt. 'If she clears this then she wins,' she told them. 'You're her friends, aren't you? I've seen you lot together.'

Before they could reply, Sasha began her run-up. 'She's really going for it,' breathed Nabila as the pole crunched into the box. 'Oh, wow!'

There was never any question that Sasha was going to clear the bar. 'She had ten centimetres to spare,' gasped Nabila. 'She's incredible.'

'It's your turn now, Maxine,' said John as an elated Sasha walked towards them and exchanged hugs with Nabila. 'They're getting ready.'

Maxine's stomach turned to jelly. As she walked over to the start her legs felt as if they belonged to someone else. They would be running the first bend of the race in lanes, and she took her place right on the outside. She took a quick look over at Jade, who had lined up in lane four, and then the starting pistol went and they were off.

Maxine forced herself to hold back, remembering the night before, but before they had gone a hundred metres she knew that she was running too slowly. When they had rounded the bend and it was time to break, all the other runners were inside her. She wasn't sure what to do. She could either keep running outside them, or drop to the back, or make a break for the front. She decided to stay where she was, a couple of metres behind Jade, but with two other girls inside her.

All the way round the second bend Maxine stayed on the outside, and when one of the girls inside her stumbled, she was forced even wider. Now she was struggling to hold her position. She fixed all her concentration on staying with Jade and barely noticed that she was being forced to run further than any of the others.

Then, as they came into the home straight for the first time, a small gap opened up behind the two leading runners, and Maxine put on a spurt to force herself into the space.

As they passed the finish line at the end of the first lap, a bell rang and Maxine felt the pace quickening. She was still where she wanted to be and she was feeling good. They were running fast, but no faster, she was certain, than she had run the night before.

And then, as they entered the final bend, two things happened. A runner tried to pass Maxine on the outside, and Jade suddenly opened up a gap of three metres between her and the girl behind her. Maxine tried to respond, but now there were two runners outside her, boxing her in behind the girl ahead of her, who seemed to be slowing up.

There was nothing Maxine could do. She had

to wait while four runners came past her before she could move out and sprint after them. By that time, Jade was well clear and looking over her shoulder at the chasing pack.

Maxine finished fourth. When she had recovered a little she saw one of the girls who had boxed her in walking past. 'You should have let me out,' she said angrily.

The girl paused, then shrugged. 'It's a race, right? You got yourself in a bad position. That's the way it works.'

Maxine started to say something else, but she swallowed the words before she spoke them. The girl was right. And now Kath was beside her, giving her a sympathetic smile.

'OK, Maxine? That was a steep learning curve for you. You probably ran fifteen metres further than anyone else. If you'd got your tactics right, you could have won that race.'

CHAPTER ELEVEN

After the race Maxine changed quickly, threw her things into her bag and returned to her room without talking to her friends. She knew perfectly well that she could have won the race, and she kept replaying the whole thing in her mind as she showered. She pulled on clean clothes and went to throw her running gear in the laundry basket. For the second time that day she found herself staring in disbelief into the bottom of her bag.

Her shoes were there, as if they had been there all along. For a moment she thought she was going crazy. How could she not have seen them? But they hadn't been there earlier. They really hadn't. She had turned the bag upside down.

Someone had taken them, and now they had put them back.

She had to admit that they had been clever. She hadn't noticed a thing. But it was definitely time to get back at them.

'I thought you did good,' said John, later that evening as they ate supper in the restaurant. 'It was your first race, after all.'

Kayle had chosen strawberry jelly and ice cream for her dessert and she was poking at it thoughtfully with her spoon.

'I don't care,' Maxine said. 'If Kath says I could have won it, then I ought to have won it.

I did everything wrong.'

'It wasn't all your fault,' Kayle said. 'It sounds as if you'd already run for miles looking for your shoes.' As she said this, she looked across at Tamsin and Melissa. Maxine had told them all about the mysterious reappearance of the shoes. 'I was just thinking,' Kayle continued. 'Imagine if you got into bed and you put your feet in a whole load of jelly.'

'That is such a good idea,' Maxine said, reaching out with her spoon and digging it into Kayle's jelly. 'You would definitely scream, wouldn't you?'

'For sure,' agreed Sasha, with a wicked grin.

'What about Oliver?' Kayle asked John. 'Would he scream?'

'Probably not,' said John, considering. 'But I reckon he wouldn't like it much.'

'Let's do it,' Kayle said. 'Let's do it now. If you all get some jelly we can put it in this plastic bag.

It's just perfect.' She pulled a supermarket carrier bag from her pocket and, with a surreptitious glance at Tamsin and Melissa to make sure they weren't watching, scraped the jelly into the bag.'

'If they've left their doors open,' John said.

'Most people do when they come to eat,' Sasha said. 'Those cards are too annoying.'

They had discovered that not everything worked perfectly at Camp Gold. It often took several tries to make the plastic cards open the doors and most people had stopped bothering.

'I locked mine,' said Maxine. 'I'm not going to lose my shoes again.'

'Stop talking and get on with it,' hissed Kayle. 'We have to do this before they finish eating.'

Sasha, Maxine and John all went back and collected plates of jelly. 'You're hungry, then,' remarked the girl behind the counter.

'Our friend had it,' Maxine said. 'It looked so delicious that we all wanted some.'

'That was embarrassing,' Sasha said as they returned to their seats and Kayle quickly tipped the jelly into the bag.

'OK,' Kayle said. 'Let's go.'

'I can't go up there,' John said, when they paused at the foot of the stairs.

'No, but you could put some in Oliver's bed,' said Kayle.

'I really can't,' John said. 'I'm pretty sure he's in his room.'

They left John standing in the entrance hall. 'I think maybe he is scared,' giggled Sasha.

'Shhh,' whispered Maxine. 'We don't want anyone to hear us.'

They moved in silence along the corridor until they came to Tamsin's room, where Kayle gave the door a gentle push. It didn't move. She reached down and turned the handle, but the door was most definitely locked. 'It's OK,' said Kayle. 'We'll try Melissa's.'

But Melissa's room was also locked, and as the disappointed trio returned along the corridor to Maxine's room they ran straight into Tamsin and Melissa. The two girls walked past them without a word. 'Phew,' breathed Kayle. 'That was lucky. They would have caught us red-handed.'

'We'll have to find another way,' said Maxine.

'Don't worry,' replied Kayle. 'I'll think of something.'

As the second week at Camp Gold began, Maxine found that she had very little time to think about Tamsin and her friends. She threw herself whole-heartedly into her training and did everything that Kath asked of her as well as she possibly could. She even found that she could have a laugh with the other girls. All except Jade.

'Don't worry about her,' said a redhead called Martine. 'She's always like that. All she ever thinks about is running.'

It was Thursday morning, and right now Jade was sitting alone, a little apart from the other girls. Maxine stood up and walked over to her. 'Why don't you come and sit with us?' she asked.

Jade glanced up at her and then returned to writing in a small black notebook. 'What is that?' Maxine asked curiously. It was some kind of chart full of neatly written numbers.

'It's none of your business, that's what,' said Jade, snapping the book shut.

'OK,' said Maxine. 'I was just trying to be friendly, that's all.'

'Well, don't.'

Maxine didn't move. Jade was really something. Then she realized that Jade was looking at her shoes, and a suspicion blossomed in her mind. 'It was you, wasn't it?' she blurted out. 'It was you who took them.'

Jade stared at her, then laughed. 'Me?' she said.

'You seriously think I'd do that? I could still beat you, whatever shoes you were wearing.'

Maxine held Jade's gaze a moment longer. Her eyes were cold and grey, and full of contempt. I've got it wrong, Maxine thought. I've got her wrong. She looked down, then started to apologize, but Jade was already jogging back to the track.

'You see?' said Martine, when Maxine rejoined the group. 'It's a waste of time.'

That night Maxine joined the others on the basketball court after supper. The evening game had become a feature of life at Camp Gold. There was a bunch of regulars, including Maxine and her friends, Nabila the pole-vaulter, and a couple of the gymnasts. Some of the coaches also came down for a game occasionally, and tonight both Michael and Greg had joined them.

'I've got some news for you guys,' Michael said as he pulled on his sweatshirt after the game was over. 'Danny Crowe's coming back on Saturday to watch the competitions. I've been watching everyone working and I'm hearing great things from your coaches. And there's another thing—'

But they never got to hear about the other thing, because at that moment Michael saw Isabel walking past. 'I'll see you later, guys,' he said, and ran off after her.

Greg was shaking his head. 'They're up to something, those two,' he said.

'We'd noticed,' said Kayle, raising her eyebrows. All the girls giggled.

'No way,' said Greg. 'That's not what I meant at all. I'm sure they're just friends.'

'Very good friends,' said Kayle when Greg was out of earshot. 'Extremely good friends. Don't you think, Maxine?'

But Maxine was lost in thoughts of her own. Danny Crowe was going to be watching on

Saturday! This was her chance to put right everything that she'd done wrong in the last race. Already she was thinking about her tactics. She knew exactly what she was going to do.

What Michael had not told them was that the TV crew would be visiting Camp Gold on Saturday. He made the announcement on Saturday morning as they were eating breakfast. 'Mostly they'll be taking general shots,' he said. 'Footage of you guys moving about the Camp and then they'll be shooting the competitions. They might want to do a few interviews afterwards, but they have to clear that with your coaches first, OK? Enjoy your day.'

Maxine took care to keep out of the way of Corenza Lewis all morning, but it wasn't easy. The TV crew seemed to be everywhere – in the gardens, on the tennis courts, by the pool and in the gym.

'You're mad,' said Kayle. 'You shouldn't be hiding. You should do what I'm doing. I've got myself into at least a dozen shots.'

Maxine laughed. 'You're the one who's mad,' she said. 'I suppose you're going to try to be interviewed too.'

'You bet,' agreed Kayle. 'How often do you get the chance to be on national TV? And with those dance moves you gave me, I really hope they want to film some of us in the gym. Look, they're filming the basketball court now. Come on, let's get in this one too.'

When she arrived at the track that afternoon Maxine could feel an extra charge of excitement in the air, like static electricity. There was a heightened nervousness about all the competitors as they shot sidelong glances at the TV cameras, but like everyone else Maxine was far more concerned about the presence of Danny Crowe.

When she first caught sight of him he was in the centre of a small group of people answering a string of questions from Corenza Lewis. He noticed her as she walked quickly past, and gave her a wave. Maxine waved back, a little shyly, and headed off towards the changing rooms before the TV camera could follow her. When she emerged a few minutes later she found Danny and Michael waiting for her. 'So you changed sports, then?' asked Danny with his infectious grin. 'If you're as good at this as you are at basketball I bet everyone will have to watch out. I'm looking forward to seeing you run.'

Maxine felt awkward and embarrassed. 'I . . . I mean, well . . . thanks,' she stammered. Then she became aware that someone was watching and she turned to see Jade staring at her. 'I'm sorry,' she said to Danny and Michael. 'I have to go and warm up.'

She went out to the field where she found John and Sasha, together with several other Camp Gold students who were keen to avoid the TV cameras as they prepared for their events. John and Sasha left quickly as both their events were starting.

Maxine continued warming up alone. She wanted to clear her mind of everything and concentrate on visualizing how she was going to run the race. Today she planned to hang back, and not worry so much about staying close to Jade. She would only move up if Jade started to open a significant gap on the others, and she would avoid getting boxed in at all costs.

While she imagined all this she jogged gently around the edge of the field. She felt good. She knew for sure that all the training had really been making a difference. All she had to do now was make sure there were no foolish mistakes. She glanced at her watch.

It was time to go.

Back at the track Kath was already calling the 800-metre competitors together. 'I know you'll all be extra-nervous,' she said, 'what with Danny Crowe and the TV cameras, but this is good practice for the big competitions I'm sure you're all be going to be part of soon. Just imagine what it's like going out for an Olympic final! Well, I'll tell you – it's like this, but a million times more scary. And a million times more exciting too.'

'You mean you—'

'Sure,' said Kath. 'Didn't you realize? Each one of the Camp Gold coaches has been to the Olympic Games. We haven't all won medals, like Danny, but quite a few of us have been in finals. And maybe you lot will too, one day. Are you all ready? Let's show them what you can do!'

The girls lined up on the track. For today's race Maxine was drawn in lane four, and Jade was outside her in lane six. Maxine sensed a hush around her, then she heard the starter. 'Take your marks . . .'

The starting pistol fired and Maxine moved smoothly away from the start. It took only four strides for her to catch the girl in lane five, and she was catching Jade too. She knew she had set off too fast, but she felt good, and suddenly she had a new vision of how the race could go.

A simple vision.

She would run from the front, and she would run faster than anyone else.

They were almost at the point where they could break for the inside lane, and Maxine made her decision. She surged past Jade and now her path was clear to the inside. As she raced down the straight she could hear Jade behind her. She knew she was going fast – almost as fast as she had run in that first four hundred with John – and she wondered if Jade would try to stay with her. As she entered the second bend she sneaked a look behind and she had her answer. There was a clear gap.

And now Maxine stopped thinking about the other runners. She felt energy surging through her. She was dimly aware of voices at the side of the track urging her on, but now she was running just for herself. She heard the bell, but it meant nothing. She ran the bend; she ran the back straight and the final bend, and never once did she slow, or falter. The finish was ahead. Now she would really run.

She had never known she could do something like this. She was running faster than she had ever dreamed was possible, and only when she had crossed the line did the exhaustion hit her. She collapsed to the ground, and after a few moments the white noise in her ears cleared away and formed itself into the babble of excited voices. Then a strong brown arm reached down and pulled her to her feet. 'Unbelievable run!'

said Danny Crowe. 'The way you ran that is just about the most amazing thing I've ever seen from someone your age. Just awesome!'

The faces around her seemed to click suddenly into focus. There was Kath, and there behind her was Jade.

Maxine just had time to glimpse the tears rolling down the other girl's cheeks before Jade turned and walked quickly away.

CHAPTER TWELVE

As soon as she could, Maxine escaped from the small crowd of people who had gathered around her after the race and made her way back to the changing room. A few minutes later Kath came in and sat down beside her. 'How do you feel?' she asked.

'I feel good. A bit shocked, I guess. I didn't know I could do that.'

Kath nodded. 'You have a big talent, Maxine.

A natural talent. I really think if you find the right coach and you work hard, you could go all the way.'

Maxine looked at Kath. 'What do you mean?'

'I mean you could do it all. Internationals, World Championships, the Olympic Games. You're fast, Maxine, really fast. So fast that it scares me a bit.'

Suddenly Maxine felt a little scared herself. Was it really her Kath was talking about? She'd arrived here two weeks ago, sure that she'd come to the wrong place; that they'd made a mistake about her. Now it seemed that maybe her teachers had been right to send her here after all. 'You'd have to keep clear of injuries,' Kath was saying, almost as if she was talking to herself, 'and you'd need good training facilities. Are there any clubs near you?'

Maxine had no idea. 'I've never thought about it,' she said. 'Can't I just go running sometimes. Does it all have to be so serious?'

'I'm sorry, Maxine,' said Kath distractedly. 'This must all seem a bit much to you. You don't need to think about all that now, do you? Come and watch the rest of the competition.'

'Have you seen Jade?' asked Maxine, suddenly remembering Jade's tearful departure. 'Is she OK?'

'Jade's a sensible girl,' Kath said. 'When she's calmed down she'll realize that what you did was exceptional. You may have beaten her easily today, but don't think that'll always happen. She's a very good runner, you know.'

Later that night Sasha, John, Kayle and Maxine were all sitting outside in their favourite spot under the old cedar tree. The sun had gone down, but it was a warm summer night and they were all talking over the events of the afternoon. There was no doubt that Maxine's performance in the 800-metres had caused a sensation.

The TV people had wanted to interview her afterwards, but Michael had refused to allow it.

'It's a good thing too,' Maxine said. 'I'd only have said something stupid. And I still feel really bad about Jade.'

'Why?' asked John reasonably. 'I bet she didn't feel bad when she beat you last week.'

'You didn't see her,' Maxine said. 'She was so upset.'

Kayle had been looking up at the front of the Camp Gold building while they were talking. Now she interrupted the conversation. 'Look,' she said. 'I'm sure that's Tamsin's window. She's left it open.'

They all looked up at the top floor where the windows were reflecting the remains of the sunset. 'But there are lots of windows open,' Maxine said. 'How do you know which one is hers?'

'Because I counted the rooms,' Kayle said.

'Hers is the third from the end. We could get in. We could change her room around. We could mess up her bed. We have to do *something*.'

'It's on the first floor,' John pointed out. 'I don't see how.'

'We can find a ladder,' Kayle said. 'There must be one here somewhere.'

'Or we could use a pole-vault pole,' said Maxine suddenly, looking at Sasha. 'Couldn't we?'

'Maybe,' replied Sasha doubtfully. 'They are very bendy, you know. Better for sliding down than climbing up, I think.'

'We have to try,' said Kayle, springing to her feet. 'It's nearly dark so there couldn't be a better time. Let's get the pole.'

They made their way down to the track and waited while Sasha ran over to retrieve her pole. 'I'm not so sure this is a good idea,' Maxine said. 'Someone could easily see us.'

'They won't,' John replied. 'They're all watching the movie.' He stopped talking suddenly and stared over Maxine's shoulder. 'What's going on down there?' he said. 'Can you see?'

He pointed down the grassy avenue that led to the wooden gate they had used to get to the sea. All Camp Gold's gates were locked at dusk, but now a shadowy figure was climbing in. The silhouette was sharply outlined for a moment against the orange sky. It was Tamsin. They heard her call softly to someone on the other side of the gate and at the same time Maxine heard footsteps behind her. She turned and saw Michael approaching. In one more second he would see Tamsin and her friends climbing over the gate. Suddenly Maxine knew that she didn't want that to happen.

'Hi, Michael,' she said brightly.

'Oh, hi there, guys,' Michael said distractedly. 'I thought I saw—'

'Have the TV people gone now?' Maxine interrupted him, desperate to think of something to say to keep his attention.

'Sure. They left hours ago. Now if you don't mind—'

'Only I was wondering,' Maxine persisted. 'Will they be here for the final competition next weekend?'

Michael sighed. 'I wish we didn't have to let the TV in at all. But obviously we have our sponsors to think of, and they insist. You lot really should be getting inside now. I—'

He made to walk on, but Kayle spoke up brightly. 'I say, Michael,' she said as three shadows slipped away silently into the gardens behind him. 'I was just wondering, was Isabel a very *good* gymnast when she was younger, because she is very *beautiful*, isn't she?'

'I . . . Well, yes,' Michael stammered. 'I mean to say, she was a brilliant gymnast . . . Not that I'm

saying she wasn't beautiful too . . . I mean, she
is beautiful . . .'

He stopped, looking very flustered. Maxine
sneaked an amused glance at Kayle.

'You lot are up to something, aren't you?' said
Michael. 'I don't know what it is, and I'm not
sure I want to know. Just make sure it doesn't
spoil all the good work you've been doing. You
all did great this afternoon, so don't blow it.
You've made me forget why I came down here
in the first place. Oh, yes. Did you see anyone
come in over that gate?'

They all shook their heads.

'I guess I must have imagined it then. See you
later.' Michael shrugged and walked off.

'We should have let him catch them,' said
Kayle as he walked away. 'It would have served
them right. I'm beginning to think we'll never
get our revenge on them.'

'It would have been the same as telling a

teacher at school,' Maxine said. 'You know we never do that. And besides, it's kind of cool that they were out there anyway.'

'I suppose,' said Kayle. 'It's a shame we couldn't get into her room, though. It would have been fun.'

They returned to the main building. The last of the sunset had faded and Sasha exclaimed as she looked back at the darkening sky. 'There is a new moon,' she said. 'Like a fingernail! In Russia we say this brings good luck.'

They all turned to look. The sliver of moon was low in the sky above the trees, and the first stars were starting to appear.

'I wonder what that lot were doing out there?' said Maxine. 'It must be amazing down on the beach at night. Do you think that's where they'd been?'

They all looked at each other. Maxine knew they were all thinking the same thing. 'If they can do it, there's no reason we can't too,' said John. 'It's easy to climb the gate, but the buildings are locked at night. We'd have to sneak out through a fire-door and hope that no one noticed we'd left it open.'

'We can look tomorrow,' said Kayle, excited. 'It's a brilliant idea. Let's do it! Put your hand in if you agree.'

They all touched hands solemnly.

'It's a deal,' said Maxine.

As she climbed the stairs to her room, she thought about the coming adventure. She felt a shiver of excitement as she anticipated the walk down to the beach in the darkness. It was hard to believe that she had ever wanted to run away from this place. And the run this afternoon – she would never forget the feeling of power she had experienced as she surged down the straight towards the finish line. Kath could talk about the Olympics, but that was years away, if it ever happened. It was the feeling that mattered.

Only – she couldn't help thinking about Jade. She pulled on her pyjamas and got into bed. She remembered how she had run from the gym in tears that day. Maybe that was how Jade was feeling. She knew it wasn't her fault exactly, but she wished she could do something to make it better.

She was starting to drift off to sleep when a noise outside her door startled her into wakefulness. She waited. There it was again! Someone was knocking very softly on her door. She jumped out of bed, listening intently. Then she opened the door.

Tamsin and Melissa stood there in their pyjamas. 'Let us in, quick,' hissed Tamsin. 'Someone might see us.'

Maxine stood back, too astonished to do anything else, and the two girls moved past her into the room. 'We came to say thanks,' Tamsin said. 'That was pretty cool, what you did out there. Michael would have caught us, for sure.'

'Yeah, well . . .' Maxine shuffled her feet. 'What else were we going to do?'

'You could have turned us in,' said Melissa. 'I wouldn't have blamed you. We've been kind of mean to you, after all. So we wanted to say sorry too. It was us who nicked your shoes.'

'I knew it!' exclaimed Maxine. 'That was so mean. And the booby trap, was that you too?'

'We thought it didn't work,' said Melissa. 'You found it, didn't you? We were worried you'd tell someone.'

'It worked all right,' Maxine said. 'But it got Kayle, not me. Actually, she looked pretty funny.'

'What do you think?' Tamsin asked suddenly, looking at her hopefully. 'Can we be friends?'

'I guess,' Maxine said. 'But Kayle might think different.'

'Yeah, I feel bad about her too,' Tamsin said

with a rueful smile. 'That girl can do some amazing things, you know.'

'I do know,' agreed Maxine. 'What were you doing tonight anyway? Why were you climbing back in so late?'

Melissa and Tamsin exchanged looks. 'Go on, tell her,' Melissa said.

'It's my birthday,' said Tamsin. 'In two days' time. We're planning to have a party on the beach on Tuesday night and we went out tonight to arrange things with our friends.'

'It's all sorted,' Melissa said. 'There's going to be a barbecue and music and a bonfire and everything. Only we got carried away while we were talking about it and we forgot about the time.'

'We thought no one would notice we were gone while the movie was on,' Tamsin explained. 'It would have been bad news if you hadn't covered for us.'

The two girls exchanged glances again. 'The thing is,' Tamsin said, 'we wondered if you'd like to come to the party. You and your friends.'

'Or maybe you don't dare,' said Melissa.

Maxine started to say something sharp, then saw the grin on Melissa's face. 'We dare, all right,' she said, thinking of their earlier agreement to visit the beach by moonlight. 'I'll tell the others in the morning.'

But when she told Kayle about her midnight visitors the next day, Kayle only frowned. 'They do all that stuff to us, and now you want to be friends with them, just like that?' she said. 'It was going to be just the four of us going to the beach. How do you know it's not some kind of sneaky trap? They'll get us to break out at night and then they'll tell on us.'

'They won't,' said Maxine. 'I mean, Tamsin said some cool things about you. I think she was just jealous because you're better than her.'

Kayle was still frowning, but Maxine could tell that she was pleased at the compliment. 'I'm better at some things,' she said, 'but Tamsin's easily the best vaulter. I still don't trust her, though. Let's see what the others think.'

When John and Sasha arrived for breakfast, Maxine was disappointed to discover that they were just as sceptical as Kayle. 'You think they've just suddenly changed overnight?' John said. 'I ain't so sure.'

'John is right,' Sasha said. 'You cannot trust them. They have been our enemies from the very start.'

'You like Oliver,' Maxine said to John. 'You told me so.'

'I think he's a great runner,' John said. 'I know he's a great runner, but that doesn't mean they wouldn't play more tricks on us.'

'I heard that,' said Tamsin. They had been so engrossed in their conversation that they hadn't noticed Tamsin and Melissa approaching. 'We said sorry to Maxine last night, so now we're saying sorry to you, OK? Right, Melissa?'

'We thought we were done for last night when we saw Michael coming,' Melissa said. 'How did you manage to stop him?'

'That was easy,' said Kayle. 'We asked him about Isabel. If you ask Michael about Isabel he can't think about anything else.'

There was a pause, and then suddenly they were all laughing together. 'So that's OK, then?' asked Tamsin. 'You'll all come to my party?'

'OK,' said Kayle. 'It sounds cool. But we'd better make very sure we don't get caught.'

CHAPTER THIRTEEN

On Tuesday evening Maxine arrived in the restaurant for supper and found John, Sasha and Kayle deep in conversation.

'We're not sure about tonight,' Kayle said as soon as she saw her.

'Why?' asked Maxine. 'Has something happened?'

'No,' replied Kayle. 'Tamsin's been really friendly in the gym, but I don't actually trust her.'

'And I also do not trust them,' Sasha said.

'What about you, John?' Maxine said.

'I guess I think it's all a bit sudden,' replied John with a troubled frown. 'I mean, I know we helped them out and all, but they were kind of mean before that.'

'I don't get it,' Maxine said. 'I'm the one they really had it in for. They said they were sorry, didn't they? They—'

She stopped talking as a sudden hush fell over the crowded restaurant. Michael was standing by the counter with his hand raised and a face like thunder. Maxine felt sudden flutters in her stomach. Trouble was coming to someone, she was sure of that.

'Last night some of you had a party in one of your rooms,' he said. 'I've only just found out about this, and as you can see I am feeling kind of angry about it. We trusted you guys, and some of you have let us down. We have a curfew at night, and you know that. So I'm going to have to get members of staff to do random patrols of the corridors, which is going to put all of them in a bad mood because we're all going to be losing sleep. That's all.'

Michael left the room quickly and there was no sign of his usual infectious smile.

'That's it then,' said Maxine. 'Now there's no chance of any of us getting out tonight.'

After they had eaten they went out to the basketball court as usual. It was strangely deserted. 'Well, I don't think Michael's likely to come after that,' said John. 'I wonder who it was had the party.'

'It doesn't matter,' said Kayle. 'It's ruined it for us.'

'I thought you weren't going to go,' Maxine said, then stopped as she saw Tamsin approaching. Oliver and Melissa were a short distance behind her.

'I thought we'd find you here,' Tamsin said gloomily. 'I can't believe this is happening to me. It's my birthday and now I can't go to my own party. My big brother's doing a barbecue and everything. It's so unfair.'

Maxine looked at Kayle and saw from the look on her friend's face that her doubts about Tamsin had gone. There was no way that Tamsin was faking, and they could all see it. And now suddenly all of them were desperate to go to the party.

'There has to be a way,' said John.

'It is true,' said Sasha, her eyes shining. 'We cannot be defeated by their foolish little rules.'

'I don't see how,' Oliver put in. 'It's all right for me and John. We can just climb out of our windows. But . . .'

'That's it!' exclaimed Maxine. 'We were talking about it the other day. We can use Sasha's pole!'

'Really?' asked Tamsin. 'Would it be strong enough?'

'Of course,' replied Sasha. 'The boys can escape first, and lift up the pole for each of us to slide down. We should fetch it now.'

'Sasha's right,' said John. 'We need to put it somewhere where we can find it easily. Let's go get it!'

When they reached the track Sasha retrieved her pole from beneath a canvas cover. 'We'd better go round the outside of the gardens,' Tamsin said. 'We can't just carry it straight up the path.'

A line of trees ran along the edge of the Camp Gold site, just inside the boundary wall, and the trees extended close to the far end of the block where the girls' rooms were situated. They made their way round the back of the running track and managed to reach the foot of the wall beneath Maxine's window without being seen.

They laid the pole in a flower bed and arranged the plants carefully to hide it.

They were only just in time. As Maxine stood up Michael and Isabel came round the corner of the building and stopped when they saw the seven students. Michael looked at them suspiciously. 'What are you up to?' he asked. 'I just know you're up to something. I can't believe you came round here to admire the flower beds.' He took a step towards the plants.

'We . . . we were looking for you,' said Kayle innocently. 'Weren't we, everyone? We were hoping you'd come and play basketball. But if you've got something more important to do . . .'

'Michael isn't playing basketball because we're making sure that none of our students are doing anything they shouldn't be doing,' Isabel said, looking sharply at Kayle.

'And believe me, I'd rather be playing ball,'

Michael added grimly. 'I think you'd all better make yourselves scarce.'

They walked towards the basketball court as Michael and Isabel headed off around the edge of the grounds. 'You don't think they know about the party, do you?' asked Tamsin as John retrieved the ball and began bouncing it thoughtfully.

'I don't see how they could,' said Maxine. Their expedition was starting to seem more dangerous with every minute that passed. 'If we'd been a second later hiding that pole, they would have caught us.'

'Well, I'm not going to miss this party,' said Kayle. 'If it was easy, it wouldn't be half as much fun, would it?'

They all agreed. 'OK, then,' Oliver said. 'The party starts at midnight. You girls be ready at half-past eleven. And don't make a sound, OK?'

★   ★   ★

Back in her room Maxine lay on her bed listening to her iPod. It was only nine o'clock. More than two hours to wait. She picked up a book and tried to read, but it was no good. She was more nervous than she'd felt before the start of any of her races, but she was excited too, as she pictured the waves breaking on a moonlit beach. Sleep took her by surprise, and she was awoken by a scratching sound.

She looked sleepily at her watch and was horrified to see that it was already eleven-thirty. She jumped up and ran to the window. Sasha and John were standing underneath and she could see their faces looking up at her, pale in the moonlight. The end of the pole was leaning against her windowsill.

John beckoned urgently. Maxine looked down. 'There's a ledge just below the window,' he hissed. 'Hold onto the pole and lower yourself down.'

Maxine saw what he meant. She turned herself round and edged through the window, dangling her feet until they found the narrow ledge below her. Then she took hold of the pole with both hands and slid quickly down, landing on the grass with a gentle thud.

'Cool,' said John. 'The others are in the trees. We'll just hide the pole.'

'What happened?' whispered Kayle. 'They were standing there for ages.'

'I fell asleep. I still feel half asleep. This is like a dream, isn't it?'

'Better,' said Tamsin. 'Let's get moving.'

Maxine knew what Tamsin meant. Behind them the white facade of Camp Gold was like a ghost building. The lawns were silver and the shadows blue and black as the group wove through the trees and finally reached the gate.

'Here,' said Oliver, making a basket of his hands. 'I'll give you a leg-up, Maxine. It's easy.'

She put her foot in his hands and suddenly found herself boosted upwards. She grabbed the top of the wall and pulled herself over, dropping down softly on the other side. As the others joined her she caught sight of a flash of silver surf in the distance. An owl hooted overhead. John was the last over the wall and he stood there for a moment, taking in the scene ahead of him.

'What are we waiting for?' demanded Tamsin. 'Let's run!'

She set off along the path and the others followed. Maxine jogged along at the back with John. She had never been in the countryside at night before, and she was surprised to find that there was some moonlight. It was dark, but she could see where she was going quite clearly. After a few minutes they turned a corner and the sea lay in front of them.

'Wow!' exclaimed John softly. 'It's even better than I thought it would be.'

The waves were glittering in the moonlight, and long lines of surf broke gently on the sand. 'There!' exclaimed Maxine. 'There's the fire, look!'

Further down the beach flames flickered in the darkness, silhouetting the shapes of a small group of people. They ran down onto the sand and went to join them. As they neared the fire they smelled the barbecue, and even though Maxine had eaten a few hours earlier she found that her mouth was watering. There were loud cries of welcome as Tamsin and her friends arrived, and a rowdy chorus of *Happy Birthday*.

'These are my friends from Camp Gold,' Tamsin said as they took cans of drink and helped themselves to hot dogs. 'We wouldn't have made it out without them.'

'You make it sound like a prison,' someone said. 'I thought you said it was cool.'

'It is,' replied John. 'But they have these rules. Like most places.'

'And rules are made to be broken,' said Kayle. 'Are we going to dance or what?'

Someone turned up the music and soon the beach around the fire was filled with dancers, the firelight casting long shadows. Maxine stayed by the fire, content to drink in the scene around her, watching Kayle show off the moves that Maxine had taught her, happy to take comfort in the heat from the fire and from her freshly made burger. After a while three of the dancers moved towards the fire. Maxine nearly said something, but they hadn't noticed her sitting there, and then she heard someone say her name. It was Melissa.

'You should have seen it,' she was saying. 'Maxine was incredible. She just destroyed the others. I really think she might be able to beat these international athletes who are coming to the competition at the weekend.'

Maxine felt herself blushing in the darkness.

Hours later, it was John who finally remembered the time. 'We have to get back when it's still dark,' he said to the others as they sat watching the moon set over the cliffs.

'Not yet,' said Tamsin. 'Stay a little longer, please.'

John stood up restlessly. 'I don't think we should,' he said. 'It's going to start getting light any minute, and anyone could look out of a window and see us.'

John's anxiety was infectious, and suddenly Maxine found that she was desperate to get moving. They finally managed to drag Tamsin away from her friends, and as soon as they were out of sight of the beach they began to run. Now Maxine could see that the sky was brightening in the east. 'Hurry,' urged John. 'We don't have much time.'

They reached the gate and Oliver helped

them over, one at a time. Maxine went last. She slithered over the wall and let herself drop down the far side.

'We made it,' she said, turning to the others.

Torchlight flashed in her face, blinding her as Oliver landed beside her. 'Is that all of you?' said Michael's voice. 'Or are there any more?'

CHAPTER FOURTEEN

Maxine awoke later that morning with a feeling of dread. For a moment she thought that she had simply had a bad dream, but it wasn't a dream. They had ruined everything.

Michael had been waiting inside the gate with Isabel and Greg. They had all stood, stony-faced, while the friends had explained where they had been.

'You don't need me to tell you how wrong

this is,' Michael had said finally. 'I thought we'd made it clear to you all that we expected you to stick to the rules. How can you expect to train hard and perform at your best if you do this kind of thing?'

'Breaking the rules once, I can understand,' Isabel said, 'but we're starting to lose count of the number of times you've stepped out of line.'

Somehow Isabel's disapproval was even harder for Maxine to take because she had always been so kind to her.

'You shouldn't blame them—' Tamsin began, but Michael stopped her.

'I don't want to hear another word from you right now,' he said. 'I'm too angry and I might say something I'd regret. We'll talk in the morning.'

'But . . . you're not going to send us home?' asked Maxine, fighting back her tears.

'I really don't know,' Michael said, and Maxine could see that he meant what he said. There was a real chance that they might all be sent away from Camp Gold in disgrace.

Maxine pulled the covers back over her head. It was too horrible. What would her family say if she was sent home? And it was worse than that. The people who ran Camp Gold knew every top athletics coach in the country. They would all hear about what had happened, wouldn't they? None of them would want to coach her after this.

There was a knock on her door and she heard Kayle's voice. 'Maxine? Are you awake? I know it's awful, but you have to get up.'

Maxine reluctantly dragged herself out of bed and opened the door. Kayle stood there, looking pale and anxious. 'Hurry up and get dressed,' she said. 'The worst thing we can do is be late for breakfast.'

'I can't see what difference that would make,' Maxine said.

'We make them see that we can be just as good as everyone else even if we have been up all night. Come on, Maxine, at least we can try.'

'Kayle is right,' said Sasha, who had been waiting in the corridor. 'We are all excellent at what we do. I do not believe they will make us go home.'

Maxine looked at the determined set of the Russian girl's jaw and couldn't help smiling. She showered and dressed and they went down to breakfast together.

As they walked into the restaurant every head turned to look at them. There was a moment's silence, and then a low buzz of conversation began again. Maxine knew that everyone was talking about them. Somehow the news had got out.

Maxine watched Kayle collecting cereal and scrambled eggs on toast. 'I don't know how you can,' she said.

'We've still got to work,' Kayle said. 'You should eat too.'

'I'm not sure I can.'

But when she started eating her cereal, Maxine found that she still had an appetite. Tamsin and Melissa joined them at their table, followed shortly afterwards by Oliver and John. 'Hey, listen,' said Tamsin, looking around at their serious faces. 'Whatever they do to us, it was a great party, right?'

Before anyone could reply, a hush came over the restaurant. Greg had entered the room and was making his way purposefully over to their table. 'Michael wants to see all of you at nine o'clock in his office,' he told them. 'And if you've got any sense you won't be late.'

They found Michael sitting behind his desk. Maxine noticed with surprise that the office had been tidied since their last visit, but somehow that made her feel even more uneasy.

Michael frowned when they came in, and fiddled with his pen as he looked down at a sheet of paper on the desk. 'This is very difficult,' he said slowly. 'You probably think that I'm in charge here, but when something very serious like this happens then it's not just up to me. There's a board of trustees who decide these things. It was their decision to offer you all places here, and it'll have to be them who decide whether you stay or go.'

Maxine's heart sank. All her hopes had rested on the way that Michael had forgiven them in the past. She was certain that these trustees would all be so old that they couldn't even remember being young.

Michael was still talking. 'We'll be meeting during the day,' he said. 'I'll see you all back here at five o'clock, and in the meantime you'd better work like you've never worked before. That's if you want to have any chance at all of staying on here. Now, go.'

Even Kayle and Tamsin couldn't think of anything cheerful to say when they emerged from Michael's office. They collected their things in silence and Kayle and Tamsin went off to the gym together. The others made their way to the running track.

Kath didn't speak when Maxine joined the group of distance runners, but Maxine could tell from her face that she was very angry. She led the runners off on a warm-up run through the grounds, and as they went Maxine saw Sasha jogging, red-faced, back towards the main building. Of course! Sasha's pole was still there! That was just about the worst thing of all. She could imagine how Sasha must be feeling.

'Tough luck,' whispered one of the others as they jogged through the trees.

'Yeah, you were so unlucky to get caught,' said someone else.

Maxine was surprised. She'd assumed that everyone was thinking the worst about them, but by the time they'd completed the run almost all the others had said something similar, or else given her a sympathetic smile. All except Jade.

Maxine had been feeling so worried about what was going to happen to her that she'd forgotten how bad she felt about Jade. It would be horrible to have to go home and not to have made things right with her. She put on a spurt and caught up with the other girl. Jade glanced sideways at her, then her serious face broke into a grin. 'I can't believe you had a midnight party on the beach,' she said. 'Everyone's totally jealous.'

Maxine did a double-take. 'You mean, you would have come too if they'd asked you?'

'Sure I would. Who wouldn't?'

'But I thought you took it all really seriously? Running, I mean. All this.'

'I do. That doesn't mean I don't want to have fun too. And anyway, you're just as serious about running as I am, aren't you?'

'I don't know. I mean, yes. I suppose I am. But they're going to send us home.'

'You're kidding. They wouldn't. Not you. You're the best runner I've ever seen.'

Maxine was so shocked that she almost stopped running. 'I thought you hated me,' she said.

Jade gave a short laugh. 'I was upset. You know what it's like when you lose. I hate losing, but I don't hate you, OK? I reckon you're good enough to beat some of these junior internationals they're bringing in to race against us at the weekend.'

'If I'm here,' Maxine said.

'Don't worry,' said Jade. 'You'll be here.'

Jade's words helped a lot. Maxine threw herself into the training routines and found that she was actually able to enjoy them. At the end of the morning the coaches called all the athletes together. 'We're going to finish off today by running some relays,' Greg said. 'I'll put you in teams. We'll mix up the runners and throwers and jumpers and try to make it fair. You can go off and practise your baton changes and then we'll have some races, OK? I'm going to want some of you to run in sprint relay teams at the final competition, so I'm looking to see how well you can all work together.'

Maxine found herself with Sasha, a javelin thrower called Lotte, and Jade.

Jade picked up the baton and handed it to Maxine. 'OK?' she asked. 'You hand it over to me.'

Maxine nodded and went back down the track. She was finding it hard to concentrate. She had just remembered that the trustees were probably meeting right now, deciding whether she was going to stay or leave. 'I'm coming,' she shouted, and set off as fast as she could. 'Go!' she yelled, when Jade was a few metres away and the other girl took off. Maxine caught up with her and attempted to push the baton into her hand, but the hand was twisted away from her and as Maxine released the baton it dropped to the ground.

'Whose fault was that?' asked Jade.

'I'm not sure,' replied Maxine. 'Maybe I made a mistake.'

'I think I might have moved my hand,' said Jade. 'It's hard to keep it steady when you're trying to run fast.'

'It is no one's fault,' said Sasha. 'We are all very bad at it. We have to practise, or we will look very foolish.'

For the next twenty minutes they tried every different combination of handover and gradually

Maxine began to feel more confident. There was just one problem. Every time Jade had to receive the baton she twisted her hand at the last moment and the handover failed. 'It doesn't matter,' Sasha said. 'You can run the first leg, Jade. Then you do not have to receive.'

'OK,' said Jade. 'Cool.'

But Greg had other ideas. When the teams assembled for the races he consulted with Kath before telling everyone which leg they were to run. 'You start, Lotte,' he said, addressing Maxine's team. 'Then Sasha, then Maxine. Jade, you run the final leg.'

'But, Greg—' began Sasha, then thought better of it. They sat together and watched the first race. John ran the last leg, and in spite of a dodgy handover where he almost had to stop dead to wait for the baton, he managed to force his way to the front just as he crossed the line.

'I am going to look so stupid if I drop it,'

muttered Jade. 'I've always been useless at relays.'

'Yeah, well, we'll have to make it work,' Maxine said. 'I know how you hold your hand out now. We're bound to get it right eventually, aren't we?'

Jade grinned suddenly. 'You're right,' she said. 'At least I hope you are.'

'I'll give you a shout when I think you should set off,' Maxine said.

'All right,' said Sasha, standing up. 'It is our turn. Let's go.'

Maxine made her way to the far side of the track and took up her position in lane four. She suddenly felt incredibly tired, and realized that her lack of sleep was catching up with her. But if she was going to be sent home she wanted to make sure that she had shown everyone the best she could do.

She heard the crack of the starting pistol and at once it was clear that Lotte was the slowest of the eight runners. By the end of the first leg all three of the runners on the inside lanes had overtaken her, and despite a neat handover Sasha was clearly in last place as she sprinted down the straight.

Maxine crouched in her starting position. It was still possible for them to win. In a relay anything might happen. Anyone could drop a baton or mess up the change. But if she could get a flying start . . .

Now! She launched herself forwards. She had to trust Sasha to catch her and plant the baton accurately in her hand. She was flying and there was the line. There was no point slowing down. If she slowed, then they would lose the race for sure. Time seemed to slow right down as she stretched her hand back, and then, at the last possible moment, she felt the cold metal tube slap into and itclutched her fingers gratefully around it.

She was already catching the runner outside her as she raced around the bend. Her legs powered her forwards and she felt as if she was accelerating all the time. She passed two runners inside her, and now there were only three ahead in the outside lanes, but as the stagger unwound, she realized that she was catching them too.

And now she could see Jade, and to her horror she saw Jade set off, far too soon!

She would never catch her. Her lungs were bursting now, and she forced every atom of her energy into her tiring legs. Just another metre. There was Jade's hand. It was twisting away from her as usual.

Maxine was ready. She slammed the baton sideways into Jade's hand and watched her streak away to overtake the leader right on the line and win the race. Maxine jogged down to the finish line and found Lotte, Sasha and Jade exchanging high fives.

Jade turned to Maxine. 'I nearly messed that up, didn't I?' she said. 'I went off too soon, and I moved my hand again.'

'No way,' Maxine replied. 'You went at exactly the right moment. If you'd left it any longer we wouldn't have won, would we?'

Jade grinned. 'You're right,' she said. 'We made a great team, didn't we?' She held up a hand for Maxine to slap. Maxine saw Sasha yawning and at once found herself yawning too.

'Oh, you're tired, are you?' said Kath. 'That was some pretty amazing running, girls. Excellent teamwork. Just imagine how much better it might have been if you'd had a decent night's sleep. Go on. Looks like you might need to take a little siesta after lunch.'

'I think she was smiling a little,' Sasha said as they walked back. 'Maybe they do not all hate us, after all.'

CHAPTER FIFTEEN

'Isabel made us work like crazy,' Tamsin said.

Kayle nodded her head in agreement. 'She didn't smile once all morning,' she said. 'And she got Madame Farage to give us half an hour of extra ballet.'

'They're going to send us home for sure,' Tamsin said gloomily. 'I'm really sorry I got you guys into this.'

'I've a feeling we might have found some

more trouble of our own anyway,' said John with a grin. 'We were already planning to visit the beach at night. And I wouldn't have missed the party for anything.'

'Thanks,' said Tamsin, smiling briefly. 'But we're going to miss the final day, aren't we? There are some top gymnasts and coaches coming to watch us. We'll never get a chance like this again.'

They all sat glumly for a moment. They were under the cedar tree as usual. None of them had felt like playing basketball or swimming, or doing any one of the hundreds of exciting activities that Camp Gold had to offer. Maxine had eaten hardly any lunch, but she still felt sick. Saturday's event was supposed to be a big celebration of everything they had achieved at Camp Gold, and she was wondering if Jade could be right. Would she really have had a opportunity of beating some of the international juniors who would be there? She would probably never get the chance to find out.

Sasha stood up suddenly, her big green eyes glittering with anger. 'This is ridiculous,' she said. 'We all did our training today. It was like normal. So why is it a big deal that we have been to a party? Don't they ever have parties? I bet they do. I will tell Michael this. I refuse to be sent home!'

None of them could help laughing. 'You are amazing, Sasha,' said Melissa.

'Why are you laughing,' she demanded. 'I am very serious. You should be too.'

At five o'clock they all made their way to Michael's office. 'Good luck,' said a couple of Sasha's fellow pole-vaulters as they passed them. As they walked away Maxine heard one of them say, 'They're going to need it.'

Her heart was beating fast as they pushed open the door to the office wing and walked down the corridor. John knocked on Michael's door. There was a pause, then they heard Michael's voice telling them to come in.

John opened the door and Maxine looked anxiously past him into the room. She saw Michael and Greg, and Kath and Isabel. Danny Crowe was standing slightly to one side, looking out of the window. As they filed into the room Maxine saw that Madame Farage was there too, sitting in an armchair. There was no sign of any elderly trustees.

'All right,' said Michael. 'I've got to tell you that what you guys did was totally out of order.'

The coaches sitting beside him all nodded. 'We just can't have that kind of stuff going on at Camp Gold,' he continued. 'Your parents have to know that you're safe, and we have the reputation of Camp Gold to think of.'

'You cannot send us home,' Sasha burst out.

'You told us yourself that you did things like this when you were young.'

'That's not the point,' began Michael, but Sasha hadn't finished.

'Danny said the same thing,' she continued. 'And there is another thing. We are all extremely fine athletes. When we have the competition we will be stars. We will make a very fine reputation for Camp Gold, I think.'

'Thank you, Sasha,' said Michael. 'That's enough.'

Sasha blushed. 'I am sorry,' she said. 'I say too much, I think.'

'You're not going to get very far as athletes if you can't be responsible and reliable,' Michael continued. 'I won't deny that you've all worked hard, but I have to know that you truly understand how serious this is. Talent isn't enough on its own. Without the right attitude, it's nothing. Do you understand? All of you?'

They all nodded. Maxine blinked back her tears and she could see that some of the others were doing the same. Michael gave a slight nod and looked down at the papers on his desk.

'But . . . where are the trustees?' Maxine asked nervously. 'I thought it was they who had to decide.'

'Oh, it is,' replied Isabel. 'And that's exactly what we are about to do.'

'You mean . . .'

'That's right,' said Kath. 'We are the trustees.'

'Then why did you make us think? . . . Oh, I see . . .'

For the first time the ghost of a smile appeared on Michael's face. 'I thought you deserved to suffer,' he said. 'To worry about whether we sent you home or not. And we wanted to see how serious you were about staying here. I guess we have our answer to that.'

'So . . . are you going to send us home?'

asked Maxine, suddenly unable to bear the tension any longer. 'We'll do our best, you know we will!'

Michael looked around at the other trustees, but Maxine could read nothing from their faces. 'If any of you had given up today,' he said, 'or if you'd complained you were too tired, or if you'd not tried your absolute best at everything, then you would have gone home. But you passed the test, all of you. You—'

'Yes!!' Maxine couldn't contain her excitement. She turned and exchanged high fives with Kayle, who was standing beside her. The others all gasped.

'Now, just wait a second,' interrupted Isabel. 'This doesn't mean we're *pleased* with you. And the fact that Michael and Danny sometimes used to do stupid things when they were younger doesn't make it OK for you to copy them.'

'But we can stay?' asked Maxine.

'Yes,' said Isabel, and it almost seemed to Maxine as though it was she who was in charge, and not Michael. 'But there are conditions. You don't put a single foot out of line, you act like model students, and you perform brilliantly at the weekend.'

'We will,' said Sasha. 'We will astonish everyone!'

At that, all the trustees finally smiled. 'You've astonished us already,' Danny said. 'But you really are gonna have your work cut out at this event. We've prepared a little movie compilation to show to everyone tonight. Make sure you're all there to watch it.'

'And make sure you've learned your lesson,' warned Isabel as they left. 'You won't get another chance.'

That evening the students assembled in the restaurant. A screen had been set up and Michael

220

had plugged a laptop into a projector. 'We wanted to show you all who you'll be competing against this weekend,' he told them. 'Just to make sure you don't think it's going to be easy.'

The first clip appeared on the screen. It showed a girl sprinting to the finish of a race with a huge crowd cheering her on.

'This is the National Youth Championships last year,' Michael told them. 'The eight hundred metres final. See the time?' he asked as a second girl, smaller than the first, with spiky black hair, overtook her in the final stride to win the race. 'She's a year older now, and even faster. You'll be running against both of them on Saturday.'

Maxine gulped. They watched more clips. A series of brilliant young athletes and gymnasts performed on the screen in front of admiring crowds. It was breath-taking. 'We don't expect you to beat them,' Isabel said, watching their faces. 'But if you're going to be great athletes one day, then you should have the chance to compete against the very best.'

'And maybe we *will* beat them,' Sasha said. 'Who knows? There might be a miracle!'

'You're right,' said Michael. 'With you lot I'm sure anything is possible.' He caught sight of John trying to stifle a yawn. 'You'd all better have an early night, I think. You've got two days of hard work, then the competition on Saturday, and after that you'll all be going home. Make the most of it!'

The next day was the best day so far of Maxine's stay at Camp Gold. All the athletes worked together like a team, training hard and helping each other.

'I'm so pleased,' Jade said when Maxine arrived at the track. 'I know I said I didn't think they'd dare to throw you out, but we were all worried. Now everything's OK.'

That evening Kayle came to Maxine's room. 'I've put all those moves we worked out into my routine,' she said. 'But it still feels like there's something missing. It's just before my final tumbles . . .'

The two girls worked on it together for over an hour.

'I think it works now,' Kayle said finally. 'Thanks, Maxine. Don't you wish you were still doing this? You're good.'

Maxine shook her head. 'I don't get the same buzz that I do from running. You saw those girls running in Michael's film. That's what I want to do. In front of all those people.'

'So you don't mind being famous now?' Kayle said mischievously. 'Remember that first day at the station? I had to make you go on TV.'

'I don't know. I suppose I don't feel like that any more. I thought they'd made a mistake, didn't I? I thought they'd picked the wrong person. But now I know I'm doing the right thing. Do you think there'll be a big crowd on Saturday?'

'Well, your family's all coming, aren't they?' laughed Kayle. 'They're a big crowd all on their own.'

'I know. I can't believe Dad's coming, and Lola too. My big sister hasn't come to watch me do anything since I was in the nativity play at primary school. I'm more nervous about that than I am about the TV cameras.'

'It's going to be awesome,' Kayle said. 'You wait and see.'

The following afternoon the two friends were together again in Maxine's room when the bus arrived with the athletes they were going to compete against the next day. They watched them walk from the bus into the main entrance, and if they were impressed by their surroundings, none of them showed it. Last off the bus were the two 800-metre runners Maxine had seen on

the film. 'She's grown,' she commented to Kayle, watching the girl
with spiky black hair. 'She looks tough.'

'She probably is,' Kayle said. 'We know they're good. But we are too. Come on, let's go and find out what they're like.'

A special reception had been laid on for the visitors and the restaurant was packed. Michael made a short welcoming speech and soon everyone was eating, drinking and talking. Maxine was determined not to be shy, so she looked for Jade and said, 'Let's go and talk to those eight-hundred-metre runners. Look, they're over there.'

Sasha was already with a small group of pole-vaulters and Maxine caught a glimpse of Kayle and Tamsin standing with Isabel next to a couple of gymnasts who seemed to be talking a lot. As she and Jade passed them, Maxine overheard snatches of what they were saying.

'Of course the World Championships were absolutely fantastic . . .'

'Tokyo is the most amazing city and the facilities were awesome . . .'

'Gina was spectacular on the beam . . . Everyone says she's going to be a champion when she's older . . .'

'They seem like they're really stuck up,' whispered Jade. 'I hope the runners aren't like that.'

They pushed through the crowd and saw the girl with the spiky black hair deep in conversation with the taller girl they had seen on the film. 'I don't know why my coach wanted me to come here,' she was saying. 'Why does he want us to race against a bunch of kids?'

'It must be something to do with Danny Crowe,' the other girl said. 'I guess it's worth it, just to meet him.'

'Well, at least we won't have to run flat out,'

the other girl replied. 'We can take it easy tomorrow.'

Maxine had felt the anger boiling up inside her as she'd listened to the girls talking. 'Let's not bother,' Jade said, turning away. 'There's no point talking to them.'

'Oh, yes there is,' muttered Maxine. 'We don't want to run against people who aren't even trying, do we?'

She stepped forward. 'I'm Maxine,' she said. 'And this is Jade. We're both eight-hundred-metre runners.'

'Yeah?' The dark-haired girl turned to them, laughing. 'Cool. I'm Marianne and this is Kelly. So you're going to race against us tomorrow?'

'That's right,' said Maxine, jutting out her chin.

'Well, good luck,' said Marianne. 'How long have you been running eight hundred?'

'A year,' replied Jade.

'Two weeks,' said Maxine. She could see the other girls trying not to laugh.

'Two weeks?' repeated Marianne. 'That's crazy. You do know I won the Nationals last year, and Kelly was second?'

'We saw the video,' replied Maxine. 'I thought you were good.'

'Well, thanks,' said Marianne. 'I'll tell you what, we'll try not to beat you by too much. See you tomorrow.'

With that the two girls went off to join their friends.

'You know what?' said Jade. 'It would be so amazing if you could beat them, Maxine.'

'Too right.' Maxine's eyes flashed. 'I would love it. But there's no way.'

'I'm not so sure,' replied Jade thoughtfully. 'I think there *might* be a way. 'If we could both get through to the final then I think I might just have a plan. This is what we could do . . .'

CHAPTER SIXTEEN

Maxine's sleep was troubled by dreams. She was racing down the final straight and she could see the finish line ahead of her. Standing on the track beyond it were her mum and dad and all her brothers. Their mouths were open, yelling encouragement, but she couldn't hear them. Everything was eerily silent, except for the sound of her own breathing, and her feet pounding the track.

And then she realized. She was running, but the faces weren't getting any nearer. The finish line wasn't getting any nearer either. The other runners began to pass her. With their arms raised in triumph they crossed the finish line, but Maxine was going backwards. The scene at the end of the track grew smaller and smaller.

She woke up, panting as if she had really been running a race. The dream had been all too real. What if it happened like that? It had happened to her before – why not today?

She shook her head, got out of bed and crossed to the window. It was three in the morning, and outside a half-moon was riding high among the clouds. Camp Gold looked like a magical place and she knew she would never forget her three weeks here. If she was going to win the race today, she couldn't let the fear of losing slide into her mind. She had to picture the whole race the way she and Jade had planned it.

That was what the sports psychologists had told them in their lectures.

And she had to believe in herself.

She shivered and got back beneath the warm duvet. Her family would be here in just a few hours, and she smiled at the thought. She was really looking forward to showing them around Camp Gold.

When she woke up next, it was light and Kayle was hammering on her door. 'Get a move on, Maxine. It's nearly eight o'clock!'

She leaped out of bed and opened the door. 'I overslept,' she said, rubbing her sleepy eyes. 'I woke up in the night. I'll be as quick as I can.'

'They'll be here in an hour,' said Kayle. 'We'll hardly have time for breakfast.'

Kayle was looking forward to seeing her parents just as much as Maxine was, and when the two of them finally arrived in the restaurant they could tell at once that all their friends felt the same. Tamsin was asking Sasha about her parents. 'They don't have to come all the way from Russia, do they?' she asked.

'Not so far,' said Sasha. 'Only four hundred miles.'

'Wow!' said Melissa. 'That's still a long way. All of ours live about ten minutes away. They've been to this place loads of times.'

For a moment Maxine thought that Melissa and her friends were being boastful and annoying again. Then Melissa blushed. 'I'm sorry,' she said. 'I didn't mean . . . I mean, my parents were amazed when they first saw Camp Gold. I bet yours will be too.'

Melissa was right. When the visitors began arriving Maxine stood watching anxiously for her parents' battered old red car, Kayle beside her. A temporary car park had been made in a field in front of Camp Gold and the local Scouts were organizing the parking. The two girls recognized Sasha's mother immediately. She had Sasha's cascading waves of red hair and was wearing a flamboyant green-and-red flowered dress. Sasha ran to her and was swept up in her arms while her dad watched, smiling.

'There they are,' yelled Maxine at last. They saw the red car coming slowly up the drive, and then they heard it.

'It sounds as if the exhaust has broken,' Kayle said. 'And look, there's my mum, right behind them.'

The two girls ran down to the car park. Maxine hugged her mum and dad and Joshua flung his arms around her knees. She picked him up. 'The car nearly blew up,' he told her excitedly. 'Is that a king's palace?' He pointed up at Camp Gold.

'No,' said Maxine. 'That's Camp Gold. It's where I've been staying. Come on, I'll show you everything.'

As they walked up to the main entrance Maxine heard the story of her family's journey. 'The car's OK,' her dad said. 'Just a bit noisy, that's all. I tied the exhaust up with some wire after it fell off. Debs followed us just in case, and she took Lola with her too.'

Debs was Kayle's mum. She was walking round with them, and like all the others, she was open-mouthed in astonishment at what she saw. 'I knew it would be posh,' she said as they walked through the gardens. 'But I never thought it would be like this.'

Kayle led her mum off to see the gym, and Maxine took her family on a tour of Camp Gold's facilities. She saved the running track for last. People had already started to gather around the edges of the track and athletes were beginning to warm up for the heats of the sprint races. Beyond the track on a grassy terrace two large white tents had been set up to serve refreshments to the guests.

'It's like you see on the TV,' her mum said. 'And you're going to run here this afternoon?'

'I know,' said Maxine. 'It's incredible, isn't it? And the TV people will actually be here.'

'So you're really good at running?' asked her dad.

'I think so. I love it, Dad. I love every bit of the training too, even when it's hard work. When we get back I'm going to join a club. I'll have to train a lot. Probably most nights, I don't know. But I want to go to the Olympics.'

Maxine stopped. All her family were staring at her. 'Well!' said her mum, breaking the silence finally. 'Camp Gold has certainly done something to you. The Olympics! And you really think you can do it?'

'I know I can,' Maxine replied. 'I'm going

to go and get changed. There will be two heats for the eight hundred metres and I need to warm up.'

Before she could get away she had to have more hugs with her whole family. Her big sister, Lola, was last. 'Well done, little Maxine,' she said. 'You go out there and show them!'

Maxine was glad to find that she and Jade were drawn in different heats. Marianne, the dark-haired girl, was in Jade's heat, and her friend Kelly was in her own – which was the first to be run. Before the races Kath called the Camp Gold athletes together.

'These internationals are fast,' she said. 'You all know the pace that feels comfortable to you, so don't get sucked into running too fast at the start. You can let them go. These are heats and the idea is to get into the final. You need to finish in the first four. Winning isn't important. Now off you go, and good luck.'

When her race began Maxine was glad of the advice, because Kelly went off very fast indeed and Maxine could feel her instincts telling her not to let the other girl get away. But she controlled herself. Kelly was soon twenty metres ahead of the chasing group and Maxine ran comfortably in fifth place until they entered the final straight and then accelerated smoothly past the other runners to qualify for the final in second place.

As she stood recovering with her hands on her hips, Jade passed her on her way to the start of the second heat. The two girls touched hands and nodded to each other. Maxine felt more anxious about Jade's race than she had done about her own. If Jade didn't make it through, their plan would be in ruins. As the race began Maxine pulled on her tracksuit and made her way round to where her family were watching.

'You lost!' said Joshua crossly. 'I thought you

were going to win. That girl beat you by miles.'

'That race doesn't matter,' Maxine said, with one eye on the runners on the track. 'Let's watch this. That's my friend over there. The small thin one. She's called Jade.'

The bell rang as the runners finished the first lap. Marianne had a clear lead. She looked back over her shoulder and slowed her pace a little, and Maxine knew that she was conserving her energy for the final. Behind Marianne, Jade was running on the inside, with several other girls outside her. 'She needs to be careful,' Maxine said. 'She'll get boxed in.'

As they entered the final bend, three girls broke away from the main group and chased after Marianne. 'Come on, Jade,' muttered Maxine. 'You have to go after them.'

But Jade was still trapped on the inside, and the runner ahead of her was slowing down. As they entered the final straight Jade finally managed to escape from the trap, but now she had five metres to make up on the runners ahead of her. Maxine's heart was in her mouth as Jade slowly closed the gap and eventually managed to overtake two girls with her final stride.'

'That's all right then,' she said, breathing a huge sigh of relief.

'But she didn't win either,' complained Joshua.

'Well, you just keep watching,' Maxine told him. 'Maybe you'll see something later on. And look. That's another one of my friends, over there in the pole-vault.'

'Oh, wow!' exclaimed Joshua. 'That is awesome.'

As they watched, Sasha rose gracefully, high into the air, and flew over the bar with room to spare. 'Come on,' said Maxine. 'My other friends are all watching. You have to meet them.'

They made their way over to the grassy bank

near the pole-vault pit and Maxine introduced them to her friends. They all had their own parents with them, so for a few minutes there was much excited talk as they all got to know each other. Maxine saw a man and woman standing a little to one side, and knew at once that they must be John's parents. The man looked exactly like John, down to the crew-cut hair and the twinkling blue eyes. He wore an expensive-looking blue suit. John's mother was a slim black woman, and she had John's smile. 'You're John's parents, aren't you?' Maxine said.

'Sure thing,' replied the man, shaking her hand with a firm, dry grip. 'And I bet you're Maxine. We've heard a lot about you.'

Maxine found herself blushing. 'John's really helped me,' she said. 'I wouldn't have started running if it hadn't been for him.'

'We saw your race, honey,' said John's mum. 'You were looking good, but I don't see how you're going to beat those internationals. John says you have a plan.'

'I hope so,' said Maxine. 'There's John now.'

They all turned their attention to the track and watched John put in a gutsy performance. He finished second, beating Oliver for the first time, but he was outclassed by the eventual winner, one of the visiting athletes. 'Tough luck, son,' said his father when John joined them. 'That was quite a race. I thought you'd catch that guy for a moment there.'

'No chance,' John said, beaming. 'But I ran a personal best, Pa.'

'That's great. That kind of speed would be useful on a football field, you know.'

'Pa!' John protested.

Maxine saw the mischievous twinkle in his father's eyes before John did. 'I'm proud of you, kid,' his dad said. 'Looks like this Camp Gold has been a real good thing. I guess I'm going to have to get used to the idea that I'm not going to have a football player in the house.'

They all watched as Sasha produced yet another personal best in the pole-vault. 'That girl's going to go a long way,' said a voice behind Maxine, and she turned to see the national coach standing on the path above them, talking to Sasha's pole-vault coach. 'Where does she live? I'd take her on if I could.'

Maxine hugged herself with excitement for her friend. Sasha joined them when the event was over and Maxine's brothers surrounded her.

'Can I do the pole-vault?' asked Joshua as Sasha's mum congratulated her daughter.

'Maybe,' replied Sasha seriously, looking down at Joshua. 'You look like a very brave boy!'

Maxine had never seen a bigger smile than the one on Joshua's face. But now someone was tugging at her elbow. It was Jade. 'It's time,' she said. 'We should go and warm up.'

'Go get 'em,' called John as they walked off together, followed by a chorus of encouragement from their families and friends. They arrived at the warm-up area, and saw Marianne and Kelly busy stretching. Marianne glanced at Maxine, then said something to Kelly and both of them laughed.

'We'll show them, right?' said Jade.

'I just hope it works,' replied Maxine, suddenly feeling terribly nervous. 'We'll both look pretty stupid if it doesn't.'

CHAPTER SEVENTEEN

'Now listen up,' Kath said to the Camp Gold students beside the track. 'These girls you're running against are the two top eight-hundred runners in your age group. I don't expect you to beat them, but with any luck they could lead you all to personal bests. That's what I'm hoping for. Good luck!'

Maxine caught Jade's eye. They just had time for a few muttered words as they walked towards the start. 'You're sure you want to do this?' asked Maxine.

'Look at them,' was Jade's reply. 'They think this is just a walk in the park.' Marianne and Kelly were laughing together, obviously not taking the race seriously. 'They think Camp Gold is a joke not worth bothering about. We have to show them.'

'You're right,' agreed Maxine. 'But even if everything goes according to plan I'll still probably have to run faster than I've ever run before.'

'Don't worry,' said Jade. 'You can do it, I know you can.'

Maxine felt absurdly pleased as she walked to her starting position in lane six. That was the best compliment she had ever received and it made her feel like she really could succeed. She glanced back and saw Jade settling into position in the inside lane. Really, it was a stroke of luck that she had been drawn there. The two internationals wouldn't know what was happening to them until it was too late, and then with any luck they would panic.

They were still sharing a joke even though all the other runners were ready, but now their coach spoke to them and they walked out onto the track, waving to their supporters as they did so. Marianne was in lane two, between Jade and Maxine, and Kelly was right out in lane eight. 'On your marks!' said the starter.

The pistol cracked and they were off. They had barely reached the crown of the first bend when Maxine felt Marianne coming past her on the inside. Kelly, too, was moving smoothly ahead. Maxine felt good. She was running easily, but she was full of nervous anticipation of what was about to happen. She resisted the temptation to look back over her left shoulder. She would see soon enough.

In another ten strides they would all be breaking for the inside, and it was now that Maxine saw Jade. She seemed to float over the surface of the track, so smooth was her running action, but she was moving very fast. As they hit the straight Jade had a clear two-metre lead over Kelly and Marianne, and as the runners slotted in behind Jade in the inside lane, her lead was growing with every stride.

Maxine knew that this was the critical moment. For their plan to work, the two internationals had to try to stay with Jade. For one awful second she thought that they were going to let Jade go, but then Marianne accelerated and closed the gap down to a metre, with Kelly close behind her.

Maxine muttered, 'Yes!' under her breath, to the surprise of one of the girls running beside her.

'They're crazy,' said the girl, but Maxine shut

her out of her mind. She had to concentrate. She had to judge her pace accurately; fast, but not too fast. And certainly not the killing pace that Jade was setting. If Marianne and Kelly stuck with Jade all the way round the first lap they would be lucky to finish the race, but that was exactly what Jade and Maxine were banking on them doing. Jade herself had no intention of finishing. She was going to drop out after four hundred metres having fooled Marianne and Kelly into running far too fast.

And the plan was working!

It serves them right, thought Maxine. If they had taken the race seriously they'd never have made such a basic mistake. They were running down the home straight now, and the three leaders had opened a gap of fifteen metres on the chasing group. The leaders were approaching the bell, and the international coach was yelling something at Marianne. Too late! thought

Maxine triumphantly as Jade's blistering pace began to slow. The leading runners passed Jade on the bend, and soon Maxine came up beside her.

'Go on,' grunted Jade. 'You can do it. They'll never keep it up.'

'Keep going,' said Maxine as she moved past her friend. 'You might catch them too.'

Maxine forced herself to be patient. They had planned the race in detail, and she had it fixed in her mind. Three hundred metres out was the time to make her move. She ran the bend comfortably. She had a good view of the runners ahead of her and she was sure that they were starting to tire. As they hit the straight she accelerated, and moved out to overtake the girl ahead of her.

Afterwards she was never able to work out exactly what had happened. The girl seemed to stumble slightly, and her foot caught Maxine's, sending her tumbling to the ground.

There was a gasp from the spectators nearby, but Maxine rolled and was on her feet again almost in an instant. She was running again, but she was last. She would never do it now. Her shoulders slumped, but then she heard a voice from the crowd. 'Don't give up, Maxine! You can still make it!'

She looked at the spectators and saw Danny Crowe urging her on. Her family were there too, all yelling encouragement.

She had never stopped running and now she realized that she was catching the main group fast. Maybe it wasn't too late. Her legs felt good. She felt good. She surged forward, passing a couple of back markers as they entered the final bend, and as she entered the home straight there were only three runners ahead of her – a Camp Gold girl and the two internationals.

But the gap was still enormous. She passed the

Camp Gold girl and now she started to feel the strain. Her muscles were burning, her lungs were on fire and she had a pain in her side, but still she forced herself onwards. She drove herself on down the straight and felt a surge of fierce elation as realized that she was catching them. There was a roar from the spectators beside the track, but she hardly heard it. The pain in her side was like a red-hot dagger, but it only seemed to spur her forward, and now she could see that Kelly was beaten. She was barely even jogging as Maxine went past her.

Now there was only Marianne to beat, but Maxine was running out of track.

All she could do was keep going. She didn't even know if she had enough strength left to reach the line, let alone pass the other girl.

Every stride was agony, but it was worth it.

It was worth it for the astonished expression on Marianne's face as she overtook her, ten metres from the finish, and powered on to win the race.

It was worth it for the cheers of the crowd and the congratulations of her friends as they surrounded her.

And most of all it was worth it when little Joshua came running up to her and yelled: 'You won!'

Kath interrupted the celebrations. 'There's someone over here who wants to talk to you two,' she said to Jade and Maxine. Jade had recovered somehow from the strain of that terrifyingly fast first lap and managed to finish the race in fourth place, nearly catching Marianne in the process.

A short distance away they saw Marianne and Kelly waiting with their coach. 'Well done,' Marianne said, holding out her hand with a rueful grin. 'We underestimated you. Both of you. That was very clever.'

The national coach had a smile for them too.
'I keep telling those two never to get
complacent, but they don't listen. I think they
might just have learned a useful lesson.'

'We didn't know anything about this place,'
Kelly said. 'But it seems like there's something
amazing happening here.'

'There certainly is,' said the coach, turning to
Maxine and Jade. 'I reckon both you girls have a
big future in athletics.'

'That's if they can keep out of trouble,' said
Danny Crowe, laughing as he joined them with
Michael.

Maxine turned to go and find her family and
found that her dad was standing right behind
her. 'What did Danny Crowe mean by that?' he
asked as they walked towards the refreshment
tent.

'About what?' asked Maxine innocently.

'You know what I mean,' her dad began, but

Kayle came running up to them with her eyes shining.

'Look!' she said. 'It's Michael and Isabel. They're holding hands. Oh no! He's actually kissing her! I can't watch.' Kayle covered her face with her hands, then peeked out between her fingers and saw Michael and Isabel walking towards them.

'Listen,' said Michael to Maxine as Kayle blushed furiously. 'You and Jade have done enough this afternoon. I had a word with Greg and he agrees that you shouldn't run the relay. That'll give you a chance to watch Kayle in the gym. I hear she's pretty special.'

He glanced fondly at Isabel as he said this, and she agreed. 'There's something else we might as well tell you now,' she said.

'You're not getting married?!' Kayle blurted out.

Isabel smiled. 'Not as far as I know,' she said.

'No, it's about a surprise party. We've been planning it ever since we arrived here. It's Greg's birthday and we're going to have a party on the beach after all this is over. You're all invited. Students, families, everyone. You wouldn't believe how hard it's been to keep it secret. Especially when I realized that one of the local Scouts I'd asked to organize us a bonfire was Oliver's younger brother! I couldn't believe I'd been so silly – I felt sure he'd tell Oliver and it would all be spoiled.'

'A party? On the beach?'

'Yeah, that's right,' said Michael, with a huge smile on his face. 'It sounds like fun, doesn't it?' He gave Maxine and Kayle an enormous wink.

'There's something going on here that I don't understand,' said Maxine's dad as Michael and Isabel walked away.

'I didn't understand it either,' said Kayle. 'But I do now. This is why Michael and Isabel were having all those secret conversations. They were planning the party. And she thought she'd ruined the surprise.'

'It sounds like a great way to end your stay here,' said Kayle's mum. 'But shouldn't you be getting ready for this competition you're in.'

Kayle looked at her watch and gave a cry of alarm. 'Why didn't you tell me?' she cried. 'I'll be late for my warm up. I'll see you there.'

They all laughed as she ran off. The refreshment tent was buzzing with activity and they soon found all Maxine's friends and their parents and sat with them over a delicious lunch. Maxine's little brothers all ate so much that she started to worry that they would be sick. Just in time, Kayle's mum announced that it was time to go and watch the gymnastics and they all stood up before Joshua could help himself to another helping of chocolate fudge pudding.

They took their places in the gymnastics hall

just in time for the floor competition. As Maxine watched the gymnasts perform their routines, she felt a sudden pang of regret. There was very little that she saw that she couldn't have done herself. She suddenly found herself remembering how she used to enjoy gymnastics. She and Kayle had had a lot of fun together.

And here was Kayle now, running onto the mat, ready to perform. Maxine saw Isabel and Michael watching from the side as Kayle took up her starting position, curled on the floor. The first notes of the music were electrifying. No one else had been bold enough to use the deep, urgent rhythms of drums and bass that Kayle had chosen. The first beats seemed to animate her body as she moved into the choreography she had rehearsed with Maxine, and once more Maxine found herself thinking: I could do that.

Then, as she watched, she saw that Kayle had taken the dance moves they had worked on together and turned them into something different, something completely new. And when she launched into a series of perfectly executed tumbles Maxine understood that she would never have been able to do this. She could never have been this good, not in a million years.

She had made the right decision. She was a runner, and if she could be half as good at running as her friend was at gymnastics, then maybe she really could make it to the top.

She remembered Sasha, that first day on the train. '*I want to win an Olympic gold medal one day.*'

If Sasha could do it, thought Maxine, then so could she. She wouldn't ever settle for less.

She was going for gold!

SIX MONTHS LATER . . .

The National Indoor Junior Championships

'And now we have the final of the junior girls eight hundred metres.'

The announcement echoed around the rafters of the gigantic indoor arena. Maxine badly wanted to look up into the stands and seek out the friendly faces of her family and friends, but she knew she had to keep focused. This was the most important race of her life so far, and she was determined to win it.

'In lane one we have last year's champion, Marianne Fielding.'

A ripple of applause ran around the arena. Maxine forced herself not to look round. She stared resolutely at the track ahead of her. The bend was tight. The track was only two hundred metres long, and it had been hard to get used to the sharpness of the turns, but in the heats she had run well. She had finished second behind Kelly, whose name was being announced now. There was more applause, and then Maxine heard her own name: 'Running in lane three is Maxine Fula.'

She was surprised by the loudness of the cheering. She gave a small wave, and as the noise died down she heard Joshua's voice. 'Go, Maxine!'

This time she simply had to look. There was Joshua, standing on his seat, yelling at the top of his voice. She waved again, then turned back to the track as the announcer welcomed the final runner. 'In lane eight, please welcome Jade Wilkinson.'

Jade had just made it into the final as the fastest loser. Maxine knew there would be no repeat of their performance at Camp Gold, but she was very glad to see Jade there all the same.

'On your marks!'

Maxine crouched down. The starting gun fired and they were off. As they came out of the first bend, Marianne and Kelly moved quickly past her into the lead, but Maxine didn't panic. She had worked hard over the winter, training three times a week at her local club, and she had learned a lot about race tactics. She settled in behind the two girls, letting them pull her around the tight bends and the short straights of the indoor track.

The pace was fast, but Maxine knew she had run faster than this. When the marker at the track side showed two laps to go, Marianne put in a short fast spurt, but Maxine was ready and she responded instantly, moving past Kelly and staying right on Marianne's shoulder as they entered the back straight.

Maxine glanced back and saw that Kelly was trailing several metres behind her. Beyond Kelly there was another gap back to the rest of the field. Maxine thought that maybe Jade was making a move, but she couldn't be sure, and she had to stay focused on Marianne.

They were in the home straight now and there were just over two hundred metres to run. Maxine moved out and accelerated past Marianne. As she reached the end of the straight she heard the bell. Now she had to push hard. She felt power surge through her as she forced her legs to move faster and faster. Still she could hear Marianne's feet pounding the track right behind her, her breathing loud in her ears.

And then as she rounded the final bend she sensed that Marianne had fallen back. As she

Although she was already playing netball for England she was told that she would be better off concentrating on athletics. The Newham and Essex Beagles coaches could see straight away that Christine had amazing talent. She had no training, but was beating girls who had been running for years. Sometimes she trained with the boys because she was so fast!

Christine won gold in the 400 metres at the Beijing Olympics in 2008 and is part of Team GB's Olympic squad for the London 2012 Olympics.

In 2009 she was awarded an MBE in the New Year's Honours list.

ABOUT THE AUTHOR

When Christine was fifteen years old, at her school sports day, she tried the 800 metres for the first time. Back then, she and her brother and sisters were always trying to outdo each other on sports days – they all wanted to be able to tell their parents that they had won an event. On this particular sports day, Christine ran the 800 metres – and won! She was chuffed to be able to come home as a winner. Nobody realized that this was only the start of her winning streak.

At the age of sixteen Christine joined the Newham and Essex Beagles Athletics Club and her talent for running was instantly recognized.

then she straightened up as the crowd applauded a magnificent victory.

She looked up into the stands and saw her whole family on their feet, cheering wildly. All her friends from Camp Gold were there too: John, Sasha, Tamsin, Melissa, Oliver and Kayle. She saw Michael and Isabel, and Danny Crowe jumping up and down and punching the air. Kath was there beside Danny, and Greg too. Even Madame Farage was there, yelling and waving her walking stick in the air.

Maxine looked down at the gold medal and she knew that this was just the beginning. There would be more races, bigger races, watched by thousands of people. And perhaps one day there would be the biggest race of all. The final of the Olympic Games.

She laughed at herself. It was just a dream, but it was a good dream.

And maybe, one day, it would come true.

came out of the bend she sneaked a look behind her.

It was a mistake. As she turned her head she moved out slightly, and Marianne made her move, bursting through on the inside. Maxine responded, and now the two girls were racing, neck and neck, for the finish.

With a final, desperate effort, Maxine hurled herself forward and crossed the line just half a metre ahead of her rival. She had won. She was the champion!

The crowd erupted. Maxine stood on the track in a daze as Marianne congratulated her and Jade came up and hugged her. She too looked delighted — somehow she had closed the gap and stolen third place.

Maxine was still in a daze fifteen minutes later as she climbed onto the podium beside Jade and Marianne to receive her winner's medal. She bent down and felt hands placing it around her neck,